My Father's Scar

STONEWALL INN EDITIONS
Keith Kahla, General Editor; Mikel Wadewitz, Associate Editor

My Father's Scar

A Novel

by Michael Cart

 ST. MARTIN'S GRIFFIN 🅜 NEW YORK

For all the Andys everywhere

Reprinted by arrangement with Simon & Schuster, Children's Publishing Division, New York

Excerpts from *The Four Loves* by C.S. Lewis, copyright © 1960 by Helen Joy Lewis and renewed 1988 by Arthur Owen Barfield, reprinted by permission of Harcourt Brace & Company and Geoffrey Bles, an imprint of *HarperCollins*Publishers Limited.

www.stmartins.com

Library of Congress Cataloging-in-Publication Data

Cart, Michael
    My father's scar / by Michael Cart.
        p. cm.
    ISBN 0-312-18137-X
    EAN 978-0312-18137-6
    I. Title.

  [PS3553.A7687M9 1998]
  813'.54—dc21
                                           97-43657
                                             CIP

First published in the United States by Simon & Schuster Books for Young Readers, an imprint of Simon & Schuster Children's Publishing Division

D10 9 8 7 6 5 4 3 2 1

Andy in Love

Andy in Love

"WHAT THE HELL!" Professor Hawthorne thunders. And a sudden shocked silence seizes the lecture hall as echoes of his voice bounce off the back wall—*hell, hell, hell* . . .

I sit in the center of the newborn stillness and survey my college classmates who were so animated a moment ago—laughing, gossiping, squeezing in one last syllable of sound before the start of class. And who now are so hushed. Two hundred students turned to silent stone by one angry outburst.

It's so theatrical I smile in appreciation and, smiling, catch the eye of Mr. Stevenson, the professor's teaching assistant, who is standing facing us at the front of the hall. Unsmiling as always, arms folded sternly across his chest, he stares gravely back at me, and then, without warning, he *winks* at me—one eyelid closing deliberately, *complicitously.* I look quickly away, feeling a hot blush rush over my face. *Mister,* hell! He can't be more than three or four years older than I am. But "Mister" he is to me and the other students because that's what Professor Hawthorne half-mockingly calls him: "*Mister* Stevenson."

As for us undergraduates, we are dignified with no names at all, unless "you" is a name—as in "you, in the first row."

"You, in the first row," Professor Hawthorne now

says, pointing an elegant forefinger at some poor slob who came in late and had to sit down in front to be singled out, "what did *you* just learn from my . . . *dramatic* display?"

"To shut up?" the guy hazards weakly and all of us watching the mini-drama laugh, a little too long, afraid of a second silence when *we* might be called on and humiliated, too.

"Quiet, children," Professor Hawthorne says with benign contempt, and we love it—puppies worshiping his shoes. He's our owner-god and every time he kicks us, we love him more.

He curls a sardonic lip at the kid and says, "There is wisdom in what you say but, alas, it's not the right answer."

He finally looks away and the poor kid, who has probably wet his pants by now, slumps down weakly in his seat.

"Anyone else care to hazard a guess?"

When no one does, Professor Hawthorne sighs and sarcastically continues: "Must I remind you that the subject of this class is that curious thing called the *novel*? The selection, that is, of dramatic incident and detail, artfully arranged to describe the story of life? What would a novelist choose to record about today, I wonder? The empty sound and fury of your gossiping? No, I think not. A novelist would choose the melodramatic but arresting gesture with which I began—the *dramatic* moment to be adorned with artfully selected details of setting and character."

A sigh of relief whispers across the room, because now everybody understands that earlier outburst was just an act. And so we can relax into routine, grabbing pencils and frantically scribbling notes as the professor continues to embroider his point. I hazard a peek at him and wonder what kinds of details I'd select if I were a writer trying to create HIM as a character?

Let's see: An American literary aristocrat descended from Nathaniel Hawthorne himself—or so campus legend claims. Independently wealthy. Movie star handsome at thirty-five with crisp, jet-black hair and eyes the color of a gun barrel. Acid wit displayed not only in class but on TV where he interviews—*interrogates* may be a better word—famous authors who, *Time* magazine claims, gladly line up for the privilege. The older professors grumble about this "star stuff"—maybe they're jealous—but the administration loves it because of the reams of free publicity it brings the university.

So Professor Hawthorne can do anything he wishes, which means limiting his teaching to this one class. Called "The Art of the Novel," it's so popular that kids begin lining up the day before registration to get in. A handful of us "gifted" students are admitted automatically, though, and here's an artfully selected detail about ME, Andy Logan: Thanks to my high school academic standing and astronomical College Board scores, I'm admitted to the class as its lone freshman, a fact I try to hide because I've learned that kids hate you if you're *too* smart. My intelligence has always set me apart from other kids but I'm like everyone else in *this* class: I'm in love with Professor Hawthorne. In the way you love God, that is: I worship him.

But today I'm glad when he's interrupted by the bell, because it signals the end of a long day—I was up at five to finish a paper for my eight o'clock class—and I really, really need my run to wake me up so I can study the lonely evening away.

I jog to the dorm, change into a pair of sweats—

it's too cold in late October for shorts—and head for the track.

Running has been my salvation since I turned twelve and in the six years since, it's become a sacred ritual. Old ladies go to mass every day. Me? I go to the track instead, where it's my pumping legs that do the praying for this lost soul.

The track I use now is next to the field where our football team practices, separated only by a mesh, see-through fence. For three quarters of each lap I can observe the purple-jerseyed jocks next door and for one quarter I can actually run with them as they pound down the field on the other side of that peekaboo barrier. On these cold afternoons in late fall, their breath rises like clouds, the ground shakes beneath their pounding feet, and the air is loud with their breathing like the sound of giant bellows. I look at them stampeding beside me, their massive chests and shoulders dwarfing the rest of their bodies, and I remember the only vacation trip my family took when I was a kid—to Yellowstone National Park—where, rounding a curve, my old man stomped on the brakes of our car to avoid hitting a buffalo crossing the road. I still remember the sudden fear I felt of the massive being that seemed to ignore us as it walked slowly and deliberately like a king but let us know through its sheer physical presence that it could hurt us if it wanted to. Even my fearless father felt that silent threat.

"Geezus," he whispered; "look at the size of that thing."

And, "Geezus," I whisper now as I eyeball *these* alien beings, "look at the size of *them.*" They tower over my six feet as the buffalo did over our car. But the real difference between them and me is not height, it's width. I weigh only one forty-five, ten pounds less than I weighed in grade school, for God's sake! I can't even imagine what these guys weigh but my eyes tell me they're twice as wide as I am—even without their shoulder pads! We seem to belong to different species and, as my mind begins to crackle and pop with endorphins, I try to imagine how my old man, the former high school football hero, would react to these modern-day giants. Would he look at them, whisper, "geezus, look at the size of them," and run away in terror? Or would he, in a desperate show of sure-to-be-fatal bravado, try to tackle them instead? Yeah, that's what he'd do, the bastard. I'm the one who would run away in terror.

I wish I hadn't thought that because my industrious mind gets busy with more memories of the old man and I try to stop them because I don't like what's being served up like a plateful of steaming brains but it's too late, the controls are frozen and suddenly I'm twelve years old again. . . .

My Father's Scar

My Father's Scar, Part i

It's 1964. Fat and fearful, I'm precariously perched
on the handlebars of my old Schwinn bicycle.
Improbably it's my father who's on the seat behind me,
pedaling; his thick legs pump furiously, his breath
comes in angry gasps. He shouldn't be pedaling so
hard, I think, but I'm too afraid of him to say so,
because he's drunk as usual and dangerous. I can smell
the beer on his breath when he swears at a car that
passes us too closely and almost makes him lose his
balance. If rage were a color, it would be the same red
as his face, and I wonder if he might have a heart
attack. It's too many years and too many beers since
his glory days as a starting tackle on his high school
football team and he's badly, sadly out of shape. Still
more years and beers later when he finally does have a
heart attack and die, the headline on the newspaper
obituary says it all: "Former Football Hero Dies."

It's the word "former" that kills him, I decide later.
Life is cruel that way. One day you're a hero, the next
you're nothing but a former. Most formers survive their
eclipse by reliving past glories through the athletic

achievements of their sons, those little moons shining so brightly in the nighttime of their fathers' lives. But I am the dark side of the moon. No light from my father's past can reach me there to be reflected back on him. Where I dwell is incomprehensibly foreign turf—as beyond my father's knowing as the dark side of the real moon. So perhaps I'm what eventually kills him or at least the disappointment I bring to his life may be what causes him to drink so much. Who knows? And who can explain why a son of his would not want to play football?

"All he wants to do is sit on his big butt and read," the old man bellows at my mother. "What the hell is wrong with him?"

It enrages him that I'm so incomprehensible and that's the real reason we're on the bike: to do something he *can* understand; to redeem me by finding my classmate Billy Curtis and teaching him a lesson. I'm to explain myself to my father by beating up the dazzling Billy, brightest moon of them all, the boy who likes to wait until we are surrounded on the playground by other *real* boys and then, grinning at me the way a coyote grins at a field mouse, ask me questions he knows I can't answer.

"Hey, Logan, how many innings are there in a baseball game? Hey, Logan, how many players are there on a football team?" Or his favorite: "Hey, Logan, how come you're so fat?"

All I can ever think to do in reply is stand there dumbly —my fat legs rooted to the spot like tree trunks, my face burning with shame—and study my shoes as if I see the answers there but in an incomprehensible language I must struggle to translate while the other boys laugh at me and poke each other.

I'm Billy's favorite target in gym class, too, when we play dodgeball. Sweatily I try to evade his shots but Billy's lithe body is a symphony of carefully orchestrated coordination and somehow he knows in exactly which direction my dodge will take me even before I do and so when I finally arrive, the ball is already there, waiting to make its stinging connection with my stomach or my head. Billy prefers my head as a target because it's harder and the ball will rebound higher from it, sometimes as high as the ceiling and the other kids will gasp in awe, and Billy will grin in unselfconscious admiration of the natural beauty of his own skill and the goodness of his life and the commanding place he holds in our sixth-grade world.

It's *his* lights I'm going to punch out. That's what my father explains to me when he finds out that Billy has been making my life miserable in these ways and worse: by lying in wait after school to back me into tight corners. Then shoving his face into mine so I can't breathe. And pushing me back into those prison-corners when I try to escape to the sanctuary of my books. When Billy has had enough fun for the day, I take my hot tears home with me and one day I make the mistake of letting my mother see them. I can't help myself. I have to find somebody who can explain to me why the whole world is a bully. Why I am so fat. Why my father hates me. Instead of explaining, instead of answering my questions, my mother simply tells my father what is going on. She does what she thinks is right but to me it's a betrayal, one that has put me here, on the handlebars of my bike, vulnerable and precariously balanced.

"Remember what I told you," my father gasps in my ear, sweat falling from his face into the dirt. "Keep your guard up. Feint. And then hit him."

I remember a picture of the old man in his high school annual—a posed picture in his football uniform, poised to rush the opposite line, looking—with his helmet on—like a bullet about to be fired. It scares me to look at that picture but it fascinates me, too. If I look carefully enough, I can see the scar on his face, the souvenir of a tackle he once threw with too much force and too little form. The referee called it unnecessary roughness. My father called it his badge of honor. The scar makes him look like a movie gangster—a tough guy.

We find Billy in the alley behind the school, the tough guy and I. We don't have to look very hard. It's almost as if Billy has been waiting for us. The old man stops pedaling. "Get off," he grunts.

"So," he tells Billy, "my son says you've been giving him a hard time." What he means, of course, is that Billy has been giving *him* a hard time. Billy looks at the old man the way you'd look at a bug on your plate in the school cafeteria.

"You're drunk," he says.

"He's going to teach you a lesson," the old man says, ignoring Billy's declaration. "Go on," he says, pushing me toward Billy before whom I stand, looking down at his spotless sneakers as shame slowly eats me alive.

"What, are you nuts?" Billy isn't talking to me. He's still talking to the old man. I might as well not even be there.

"Go on," the old man orders me. "Hit him. Show him. Beat the shit out of him."

"Yeah," Billy grins. "Show me."

What do I have to show him? I stand hopelessly in front of him, my arms dangling uselessly at my sides.

"Hit him," the old man screams. "Fight, the way I showed you. C'mon."

The old man is into it now, punching the air. Like an overinflated red balloon, the skin on his face is stretched so tight I think it might explode and spray his brains all over the alley.

"Show 'im," he shouts.

"Shit," Billy sneers, "what's *he* gonna show me—how to overeat?" He looks at me contemptuously and makes mocking, grunting noises. "Pig," he says. "Pig, pig. Go and eat your slops, piggy. I'm busy." He starts to turn away dismissively just as I, who can't bear it anymore, swing wildly at him, the punch catching his left ear.

"Shit," he says. "That hurt." And he decks me. One elegant punch and I'm flat on my back, seeing stars and tasting blood. Billy is standing over me, rubbing his ear, as furious now as my father.

"Get up," he orders.

"Get up," the old man screams, making a weird echo.

"Get up," they both command. But I don't. I can't. I'm drunk now, too, with fear and shame at what I have done and so I crawl away, instead. Out of Billy's range. Crawl to my father. Do I think he will protect me? Comfort me? Tell me it is all right? Call me "son" or "my boy"? My drunk, furious, frustrated, failed-by-his-fat-son-who-can't-show-anybody-anything father? I struggle shakily to my feet. And he kicks me. Right in the butt, as if I'm not a human being but a football. That's the thought that streaks across my mind, tumbling end over end, like a football itself, badly but strongly kicked. Will my heavy body clear the goalposts? The thought flies faster than my body can fall. But then my mind always works faster than my sluggish body. Flying, swiftly soaring thoughts. Blink my eyes and they're gone even while my body is still falling—sagging, really, to the earth—to a patch of gravel in the alley, to the sharp and individual stones—there, my hands finally engage them. Thud. Grunt. I will have scars on my palms even after I grow up. Little souvenirs of my magic moment with my father and Billy.

"Coward." It's the old man, not Billy, who says it this time. I look up at him, astonished at the reality of what he has done. My father has kicked me. Not as if I'm a football but as if I'm a stray dog, a mutt, a homeless mongrel.

Almost as if I'm appealing to *him* to confirm the reality of this unthinkable thing, I look at Billy and see—for just a second—something that looks like pity but then his bravado comes storming back, his standing-still swagger.

"Hey," he yells, but not at me. At the old man. "Pick on somebody your own size."

Taken by surprise, the old man stumbles for words. The best he can do is a frustrated "yah." Then, as Billy turns and begins to run off at an easy, I'm-not-afraid-of-you pace, the old man rallies. "I can whip your old man," he yells after Billy. "I can whip his ass."

And, wait a minute, I think, I'm the kid, I'm the one who's supposed to say that. But I don't have the energy to wonder. I'm heading home. I don't cry until I get there, though.

"He kicked me," I sob to my mother. "He hates me."

"Shhh," she urges, her hands busy in dishwater and her face pinched with anxiety, looking as if she expects the old man to pop up out of the drain any second and kill us both.

"He doesn't hate you," she soothes. "He's your

father" —as if fathers don't ever hate their sons. "He was just angry. What did you do to make him angry?"

Now it's my fault. But I tell her anyway.

"Oh, Andy, he's just concerned about you. He wants you to be able to defend yourself."

"He hates me," I sob, wanting comfort not counsel.

And getting none.

The next day I begin to run.

• • •

The first day I run until I puke and then, wiping my mouth off on my T-shirt, I run some more. I run every day after that, through pain and rain, with desperate determination. But no matter how fierce or fast my feet might fly, they can never outrun the memories I carry everywhere on my shoulders like some weird, mis-shapen, and grieving kid. . . .

Andy in Love

Andy in Love

Finishing mile six, I jog off the track and almost run into Mr. Stevenson. "Oh, shit," I think, knowing it's too late to pretend I haven't seen him standing there but not having a clue what to say, since this is the first time we've been face-to-face outside of class—the exalted grad student and the stupid freshman.

A bashful "hi" is all I can summon.

He looks me up and down so carefully I expect him to slap a sticker on me that says, "Inspected by Mr. Stevenson."

"A runner, huh," he says. "That explains why you're so"—he pauses, looking for the right word, I guess—"*wiry.*"

It's not a question but I provide an answer anyway:

"I like the exercise."

"*Mens sana in corpore sano,*" he says coolly.

"A healthy mind in a healthy body," I translate. Does he think he can impress me with this Latin crap?

"Smart kid," he says approvingly, like he's a hundred years old instead of twentysomething.

"I learned some Latin from my Uncle Charles," I say, feeling the obscure need to explain and disliking myself for it.

"I saw you in class," he says. "You seemed to think Hawthorne was pretty funny."

"You did, too," I answer cautiously, feeling paranoid as I remember he's the professor's T.A. and wondering if he has been sent to wipe that smile off my face.

"Yeah," he says with a grimace, "he's a regular Oscar Wilde in training wheels."

"If you don't like him," I say stiffly, "why do you work for him?"

"I'm not paid to like him, and anyway maybe you've heard: No man is a hero to his T.A."

There is something arrogant about him that makes you want to argue with him. Or smack him.

"Well, *I* like him," I say defensively.

"Some do," he answers shortly and then, nodding at the track, he says, "So do you run around in circles every day?"

"Rain or shine," I reply. I glare at him.

He grins back at me insolently.

"Well, see you around then," he says.

And saunters off.

"Bastard," I think.

And head slowly back to the dorm, wondering what *that* was all about.

• • •

The following Saturday I sleep late. I live in a small dorm occupied by freshmen scholarship students who, like me, have to keep their grades up and are so busy studying they don't have time to hang out. And besides we all have private rooms, which is great; it means we can study all night if we want to without bothering anybody or sleep all the next day without *being* bothered. I feel sorry for kids who have to room with strangers—

loudmouthed guys with bad breath who brag about all the girls they boink and then get mad when you don't believe them.

When I finally get out of bed around noon and wander down the hall to take a leak and a shower, I wonder where everybody is; even for our dorm it's unusually quiet and then I remember: It's Homecoming and everybody must be over at the stadium cheering for the home team. Everybody but me. I take a long, hot shower, brush my teeth, and get dressed in my oldest pair of Levi's and a soft flannel shirt, all the while pretending I'm the last man on earth and it feels kind of great, actually, until I discover that I really am the only one in the dorm and then I start to feel a little lonesome, so I pull on a jacket and head for the library.

It's a gorgeous fall day, so perfect it seems like a cliché: the sky is cobalt blue and so cloudless it looks like a canvas that has been stretched tight and painted. The trees are a riot of noisy colors, so loud you expect to hear Mother Nature telling them to pipe down already, while the air is pungent with the sweetly nostalgic smell of wood smoke and burning leaves.

The wind kicks up and blows leaves around my feet. Chilly suddenly, I sprint toward the library. I take the steps two at a time, pull the massive wood door open, and step into the quiet warmth inside.

With its vaulted ceilings, stone floors, lead glass windows, and Gothic arches everywhere, the library resembles a medieval castle, and the long wooden tables in the reading room look like knights should be sitting at them, drinking flagons of ale and throwing bones over their shoulders to dogs who catch them in midair.

Today, though, almost no one is sitting there

except for some bored-looking grad students and a few tech weenies with their slide rules.

Showing my student I.D. at the desk, I head into the stacks. They're my favorite part of the building because the books are there—stack after stack looking like floor-to-ceiling mileposts measuring your progress on the road to somewhere. I wander aimlessly along, no destination in mind, just loving the books I pass with my eyes and half-expecting to run into the ghost of Uncle Charles, my old man's long-dead great-uncle, a book lover and collector who was the odd man out in MY family—until I came along, that is.

Requiescat in pace, Uncle Charles, I think—a little ritual of mine—and, turning a corner, run into Stevenson.

Literally.

He drops the books he's carrying, we both bend over to pick them up, and knock heads instead.

"Meeting cute hurts," he mutters. "You have a hard head."

"So do you," I say, rubbing mine.

I look at him. Standing so close, I'm surprised to discover he's no taller than I am. He's heavier, though, but solid and well proportioned; like mine his hair is blond but long; it falls into his eyes which, also like mine, are blue but his are flecked with green.

He pushes his hair back.

"So why aren't you at the big homecoming game," he demands.

"Why aren't you," I counter.

"I don't have to be; grad students get a Papal dispensation."

I smile in spite of myself.

"My God, Doctor," he says with mock surprise; "the creature smiles; it has emotions."

"You should talk," I say; "you look like the grim reaper."

"So would you, Sonny, if you were Hawthorne's T.A."

I frown. And wonder why I had begun to like him.

He studies my frown. "Oh, yeah," he says. "I forgot; you have a crush on him."

"That's stupid," I say. Now I'm mad and I start to walk away.

"Wait," he says. "I'm sorry."

He sounds sincere and I stop.

"So," he says, after an awkward silence, "why *aren't* you at the big game having fun with all your little pals."

"Football's not my idea of fun," I say, annoyed by his patronizing tone. "And besides, I don't have any little pals."

"Why not?"

"I don't need any, okay?"

"Now, now," he chides, "don't get mad; get friends instead. No man is an island entire of itself."

I don't like his questions or his suggestions and so I say, shortly, "Are you done?"

One corner of his mouth turns up. "Clever boy," he says, and I realize I've made a pun without intending to.

"Here's another Donne—uh, ONE for you," he tells me coyly and recites:

'*What have you done, you there*
Weeping without cease,
Tell me, yes you, what have you done
With all your youth?'

"That's Verlaine, not Verdun," he says. "Think about it."

He gives me the same kind of half-bow Uncle Charles used to give Grandma Logan, but adds a wink and an over-the-shoulder *Au revoir* as he strolls away.

I watch him go and now I feel really lonely. I sink into a study carrel by a window so narrow Robin Hood might have shot arrows through it at the Sheriff of Nottingham. I stare out at the empty autumn day and think about the lie I've just told Stevenson, the old familiar lie I've been telling myself endlessly since I was a little boy. "I don't need any friends," I say, trying to make it sound brave and tough but knowing all the time that just speaking the words can't make them so; my heart is still the friendless loser. I sigh and lean my forehead against the cool glass of the window and find myself thinking about Uncle Charles. . . .

A Friend Of The Heart

A Friend Of The Heart

Whenever I think of Uncle Charles, it's Grandma Logan, my father's mother, who comes to mind first. And it's not a smiling, apple-cheeked grandma I see then, serving up food and love with dimpled arms. Instead, it's a grim-faced, middle-aged woman, I see, down on her hands and knees, muttering and furiously scrubbing the kitchen floor with soap that smells like a hospital.

"More hot water," she orders. It's me she's bossing. Whenever I visit, she puts me to work, Grandma's little helper.

"Don't make me wait," she snaps. "Idle hands are the devil's workshop."

If they are, the devil is out of business when *she's* around, I think sourly, handing Grandma her refilled bucket and noting she's got her working clothes on—an old pair of my long-dead grandfather's khaki pants and one of his faded blue work shirts. Her hair is cut short like a man's, its blunt ends, looking like they've been chopped off with a butter knife instead of cut by a pair of scissors, are plastered to her forehead with sweat.

"Well, don't just stand there, get me some clean

rags," she commands, adding—for my benefit—"a man may work from sun to sun but a woman's work is never done."

Neither is mine when I'm here, I want to crack, but I don't dare. For as with everything Grandma says, she has made it sound like a challenge she dares me to accept. I'm afraid to, of course—even the devil would be afraid of Grandma—and once again she plunges her scrub brush into the pail of soapy water just as there is the unexpected sound of a cough. She looks up, frowning at the interruption and its source: not the devil but an old man, instead, standing in the kitchen doorway. He's tiny, no taller than my grandmother, who scarcely tops five feet herself, but he seems smaller, perhaps because he is paper-thin while Grandma is thickset and solid as a potato. Even though he's casually dressed in house slippers, an old-fashioned shirt with a detachable collar, and trousers so often worn they're shiny in the seat, the man is oddly elegant and his voice is deep as an orchestra of bass viols.

"I don't suppose," he says, "that I might be permitted passage to the sink?"

My grandmother looks over her shoulder at the expanse of wet, freshly scrubbed floor between her and the sink. "Not if you value your life," she replies shortly.

He thinks about this for a moment and then, giving her a little half-bow and saying, "I thought not," turns and leaves the doorway. My grandmother grunts and, pausing only long enough to wipe the sweat off her forehead, resumes her work. "That man," she mutters.

It's as if I have just witnessed an obscure contest between "that man" and my grandmother and she has won . . . this time.

The man who has lost . . . this time . . . is Charles

Augustus Abbott, my grandmother's uncle —and there-
fore my great-great uncle. He occupies the rooms on
the second floor of the house. They are, as he elaborately puts it, his castle, his keep and his sanctuary.

Uncle Charles is a lifelong bachelor. When people
are occasionally rude enough to ask why he never married, he doesn't dignify their question with an answer.
But even at eleven I think *I* know why: It's because he
loves the words in the books he collects more than the
women he doesn't. He's a verbalizer not a womanizer,
my Uncle Charles. His upstairs rooms are lined with
books full of words—more words than the number of
jewels in Ali Baba's cave, I thought, the first time I saw
them.

It was that same year I was eleven. In my whole
life until then I don't suppose I had said more than a
dozen words to Uncle Charles, for he was notorious in
his belief that children should be neither seen *nor*
heard. On the rare occasions when he came downstairs, I was as invisible to him as the rest of the furniture. Mother said he was a recluse. I don't know about
that; I only know that in his selective absence from the
life surrounding him, he was an endlessly intriguing
mystery to me, like a character in a book I had heard
about but hadn't yet read myself. And so I was totally
unprepared for what happened the afternoon I was sitting in a big leather chair in my grandparent's living
room reading a copy of the *Arabian Nights* I had just
borrowed from the public library. This time it was Uncle
Charles's turn to be invisible, for when I read, I left the
real world far behind. Now I was thousands of miles
away from Grandma's rambling old house on Morgan
Hill; I was looking over Ali Baba's shoulder as he whispered "Open, Sesame!" and gasping, with him, at the

treasure trove revealed by the cave door's opening. I wasn't even aware that Uncle Charles was in the same room with me until he said not "Open, Sesame!" but, instead, "What is this? A boy and a book in THIS house?"

He sounded more than disbelieving; he sounded dumbfounded.

I looked up from my book, disoriented and equally disbelieving. This was not Ali Baba but someone who, in the mystery of his eccentricity, was even more fabulous.

"Uncle Charles?" I said tentatively.

"What is this you're reading?" he asked, taking the book from my hands and looking at it.

"Ah," he said, "and with the Dulac illustrations, no less. An excellent choice." He looked from the book to me.

"You're Harold's boy, aren't you?" he asked.

"Yes, sir," I answered.

"And you like to read?"

"Yes, sir," I repeated.

"*Mirabile dictu,*" he muttered, "will wonders never cease. What is your name, boy?"

"Andy," I replied shyly.

"And how old are you, Andrew?" he asked, automatically formalizing my name.

"Eleven," I answered.

"Eleven, eh?" Uncle Charles looked at me deliberately for a long moment before reaching a decision that he expressed as a question: "Would you like to see *my* books?"

I couldn't believe what I was hearing. An invitation to Uncle Charles's rooms was even better than hearing an "open sesame" at the door of Ali Baba's cave. Unlike my uncle I needed no time for deliberation. "Yes, sir," I answered eagerly.

"Well, come along then," he said and, without another word, led me upstairs to the waiting trove of treasure.

•　•　•

Turning right at the top of the stairs, Uncle Charles led me into a high-ceilinged room as wide as the whole front of the house. Aside from the interruption of two narrow windows and a fireplace, all the walls were solidly lined with floor-to-ceiling, built-in bookcases. The bewilderingly varied colors of the book spines made the walls look as if they were covered with exotic gems.

It was a late fall afternoon when I first saw that wonderful room, and the light streaming in through the windows was golden like old coins. It spilled over the faded oriental rugs and cast a knifelike sliver of daytime across an old globe. Next to the fireplace stood a worn leather armchair and, in front of it, a wrinkled ottoman. A side table holding a book and a teacup stood next to the chair along with an iron floor lamp with a shade made of parchment like an ancient map. In the middle of the room was a long wooden table, its surface covered with more piles of books.

I had never seen so many books outside the public library. At home all we had were a few dusty volumes of Reader's Digest Condensed Books. It was a whole new world Uncle Charles was showing me—a world of words.

"It's wonderful," I said, and realized I was whispering like I was in church or something.

Uncle Charles smiled at me—the first time I had ever seen him smile. "So it is," he agreed, sounding pleased like he was my teacher, and I had just given him the right answer on a test.

"I've lived in this room for more than fifty years, Andrew, and each time I come into it, I feel as if *I* have just come into that cave of old Ali Baba's. Well, well, let's look at some of *my* treasures, shall we?" And putting a hand on my shoulder, he guided me to the nearest wall of words.

•   •   •

I don't know how long I stayed with Uncle Charles that first day, but it was dark when I finally got home and discovered I'd missed supper. My mother was anxious and my father, drunk and angry, hollered at me, of course, but for once I didn't care. I was too happily intoxicated myself with the memory of Uncle Charles's wonderful world. And like a drunk who desperately needs another drink, I couldn't wait to return to the source of my new addiction. I began stopping at Grandma's house almost every day after school to visit Uncle Charles.

He never seemed to be surprised to see me; he never even said hello. He just glanced up from his book, said, "Listen to this, Andrew," and began reading aloud. No one had ever read to me before, but even if they had, it would have been a meager experience compared to the abundance that Uncle Charles's voice provided. It was like hearing a musical instrument playing the words, or—as he changed pitch, volume, and inflection—like a whole orchestra. In the complex sonorities of Uncle Charles's voice, language became a musical score being brought to harmonious life. I flopped down on the carpet, lay on my stomach, and listened, enraptured.

Other times I would find him standing in front of a

bookcase examining a particular volume. "Look at this," he would say, beckoning me to his side, "Isn't this beautiful?"

I would look at the book but I would also cheat a glance at his hands, which to me, were as beautiful as what they held. His fingertips skimmed the surface of the leather binding like pale birds' wings gracefully skimming the surface of a shining pond. Or gently cradling, they turned the book into a newborn baby. I had never dreamed that books could inspire such love or that love could be manifested with such grace.

The best times, though, were when we just sat and read, liking what we were doing . . . and liking each other. Occasionally I would glance up from my book and wonder at how different Uncle Charles's face looked when he read. It was like a warming light had gone on behind his eyes. And when he looked up from his own book to glance at me, the light spilled out onto his smile. At first I didn't know why this made me feel so good until finally I realized it was because it showed his approval of me and of what I was doing. So different from my father, my disapproving father whom I could never please. . . .

"Get off your lazy butt," he would storm, coming home to find me reading. "Get outside and do something."

Did that mean that reading was doing nothing, I would wonder but would be too terrified to ask.

"Go on," he would order, as I hesitated, "what the hell's wrong with you. . . ."

"What is wrong with you, Andrew Logan?" my grandmother asked tartly. "Where is your mind? Look at the spots on these glasses."

"I'm sorry," I mumbled.

"Sorry is the job you're doing," was her sour reply.

My job today was washing dishes while Grandma dried them. She had caught me earlier that afternoon when I was trying to slip upstairs unseen.

"Where do you think you're going?" she demanded.

"To see Uncle Charles," I replied, angry at myself because I sounded guilty, like I was doing something wrong.

"Leave him be," she said, "and come help me."

"But I want to see Uncle Charles," I protested weakly.

"It won't kill you to help me for once," she said grimly. "There's work to be done down here. And besides, you spend too much time with that old man. It's not natural. Don't you have any friends your own age?"

"No, ma'am," I mumbled, feeling the hot blush creeping up the back of my neck. As usual, Grandma had made me feel it was my fault that I was fat and clumsy and—worse—the best student in my fifth-grade class. Worst of all, though, the years of tiptoeing around my father had turned me into the kind of quiet, obedient, desperate-to-please kid whom teachers love—and other kids hate.

"Fatty, fatty, two-by-four," Eddie Adams taunted me on the playground. Eddie, who had unruly red hair and a rusty veneer of freckles, went to my church.

"Couldn't get through the bathroom door," he continued, chanting his favorite refrain that I knew by heart, I'd heard it so many times before.

"Why are you so full of the devil?" our Sunday school teacher, Mrs. Walker, had wearily demanded of Eddie one Sunday when she caught him pinching me during prayers. "Who me?" Eddie had said innocently, pinching me again when she looked away. But harder, this time.

"So he did it on the floor, licked it up and did some more," Eddie concluded. He was full of the devil all right and he had a pitchfork for a tongue.

The other kids, who had formed a circle around us, shrieked with laughter. And me? I did what I always did. I ran away. And—blinded by my hot, stinging tears—ran right into our teacher, Miss Flannegan.

She was wearing a hat, gloves, and her black coat with the fake-fur collar. She had been a teacher forever; she'd even taught my parents back when time began. The younger teachers wore jackets or sweaters on the playground. But not Miss Flannegan—she was all dressed up like she was going to a funeral.

"Don't let them bother you, Andrew," she said primly, "they're just jealous of your fine mind." She patted my shoulder with a black-gloved hand and then, to complete my humiliation, dried my tears with her lace handkerchief while the other kids watched, grinning, from a distance.

I wished I were dead. . . .

My grandmother threw her dish towel down in disgust.

"You're going to have to wash all these glasses again, young man. I'm going out to sweep the front porch, and when I get back, I'd better not see anymore spots."

● ● ●

I was just rinsing the last one a second time when I heard my grandmother's sharp-edged voice, sawing the air.

"Andrew," it rasped. "Come here. Right now."

I put the glass down and ran obediently to the front door.

"Look there," my grandmother commanded, as I came out onto the porch. She was pointing at an old man who, carrying an armload of books, was shuffling uncertainly by on the sidewalk.

"There," my grandmother said, as if she were accusing him of some unpardonable sin, "is the laziest man in town."

As usual when making a point, she was speaking in a voice so loud I could imagine a sudden stirring of dead bodies in Mount Olive Cemetery three blocks up the hill. Since he was only about thirty feet away, it was obvious the old man heard every scathing word. He clutched his books more tightly to his chest and, like an ancient turtle being attacked by a vicious dog, seemed to pull his head into his shoulders.

"That man," my grandmother continued, as relentless as a killing frost, "has never worked a day in his life. Not one!"

Attempting to ignore my grandmother was like trying to ignore a steamroller an inch from your heels. The old man shuffled faster but Grandma was gaining. Before she could flatten him, though, another voice, even louder than hers, erupted behind me.

"AVE, HORATIUS!"

I jumped. I hadn't noticed Uncle Charles come out onto the porch.

The old man stopped and turned back toward us. "Carolus?" he quavered uncertainly.

"Io," Uncle Charles hollered. "Quo vadis?"

The old man smiled faintly. "A scriptorium," he replied, holding up his books in evidence.

I looked uncertainly from the old man to Uncle

Charles and back again, wondering what they were saying.

"It's Latin," my grandmother volunteered, sounding annoyed. "Very simple Latin," she added nastily.

"*Touché*, Hannah," Uncle Charles said evenly, adding, to me, "that's French, Andrew, not Latin."

My grandmother snorted.

"Come and have a cup of tea with me, Horace," Uncle Charles called.

"With pleasure," the old man smiled more broadly and started shuffling toward the porch.

My grandmother shook her head, as if she couldn't believe that the laziest man in town was actually coming to her house. And, perhaps to counteract his bad influence, she went back to work but sweeping so vigorously now that she sent great clouds of dust billowing across the porch.

Uncle Charles and I stepped out of range.

"Be a good boy, Andrew, and make us some tea," he said, adding dryly, "I suspect we will need something wet to settle the dust."

When I took the tea things upstairs, I found Uncle Charles and the old man sitting together, beaming at each other like two ancient suns at twilight.

"Andrew," Uncle Charles said, as I put the tea tray down, "I want you to meet Horace Biddle. Mr. Biddle and I have been friends, man and boy, for—oh, dear—how many years, Horace?"

"It will be sixty-five years on the twenty-fifth of next month," Mr. Biddle replied with surgical precision, cutting a perfect slice of lemon for his tea.

"Leave it to a historian to have such a command of chronology," Uncle Charles said admiringly, adding for my benefit, "Mr. Biddle is our town historian."

"Unofficially so," Mr. Biddle said hastily. "Unofficially so."

He shook my hand gravely, as if I were a visiting scholar.

"How do you do, young man?"

His handshake was warm and dry and surprisingly firm.

"Your uncle tells me that you are a great reader."

"Indeed he is," Uncle Charles affirmed, helping himself to some tea.

"Good for you," Mr. Biddle observed. And then, looking around the room, he added, "I see that the apple has not fallen far from the tree. Or should I say 'the book from the shelf'?"

He winked at me, making me blush, and then he smiled at Uncle Charles. And then both men beamed again—not at each other this time but at me, instead! At me! I basked in their adult approval, as warm as the toast I'd brought them with their tea.

Uncle Charles was the first to look away, to sigh and then half-jokingly to caution Mr. Biddle, "For the boy's sake you'd better not let our Hannah hear you say that."

"Oh, dear," his friend replied. "Still the uncrowned queen of disapproval, is she? After all these years?"

"Unbowed and unmellowed," Uncle Charles confirmed and then turned to me to explain, "Your grandmother, Andrew, has always disapproved of anyone who uses his brain for more than a doorstop."

His voice sounded bitter. Hearing it, he immediately sighed again and explained, "You see, Andrew, I'm quite prepared to accept your grandmother's eternal disapproval when I'm the target, but I refuse to tolerate it when it is the occasion for rudeness to a friend.

That's why I launched that Latin exercise—my only means of retaliation these days is to annoy her."

He glanced at Mr. Biddle and—grinning like a boy—said, "I think I succeeded rather well."

"Handsomely," Mr. Biddle nodded in serious agreement. "Although I must admit I'm glad we didn't have to extend our exchange much further. I don't know about you but I find I've forgotten most of *my* Latin." He smiled ruefully. "And much of everything else for that matter. My mind is a *tabula rasa* these days."

"Welcome to the golden years," Uncle Charles said ironically. "Though I seem to remember we could converse in it for hours when we were boys." He shook his head. "Well, those days are as dead as the language itself, I'm afraid."

"Perhaps this young man will take it up," Mr. Biddle nodded at me. "Then all three of us can annoy Hannah."

"Now there's a happy thought," Uncle Charles replied. He grinned gleefully at the idea and, for a second, looked almost boyish again. But then he frowned and was old once more. "Don't listen to this, Andrew. Old bones are brittle and old men are bitter. I'm being much too hard on your grandmother."

"On the contrary," Mr. Biddle corrected. "If anything, you've always been too easy on her. I, on the other hand, will never forgive her for HER intolerance—especially when you were named poet laureate."

He grew red in the face at the memory.

"Oh, that's a long time ago," Uncle Charles said with a dismissive wave of his hand.

"Perhaps, but that's one thing I *do* remember as if it were yesterday," Mr. Biddle snapped.

He turned to me. "My ambitions never extended beyond the city limits, Andrew, but your uncle here—well, did you know he once had the honor of serving as poet laureate for the entire state? It's true," he said, seeing my look of surprise. "He did; he did, indeed, and acquitted himself with great distinction."

"They retired the office immediately after my term expired," Uncle Charles said mildly, taking another sip of tea.

"That had nothing to do with you, Charles," Mr. Biddle replied reassuringly, "only with the fact that politicians have no more soul than—well, than Hannah."

Turning back to me, he continued: "I wish you could have been present for your uncle's inauguration ceremony. It was a grand occasion."

"Oh, don't bore the boy with ancient history," Uncle Charles protested, looking embarrassed.

"History is my muse, remember?" Mr. Biddle countered. "And besides, the boy should hear this."

Uncle Charles rolled his eyes to the ceiling and turned back to his teacup as Mr. Biddle continued: "Imagine a hot July day forty years ago. We journeyed by train to the state capital for the ceremony, your uncle and I. It took place on the glorious Fourth and your uncle's oath of office was administered by the chief justice of the State Supreme Court, an imposing man with a huge white mustache. The governor was present, too, as I recall."

"Not so imposing," Uncle Charles murmured, "a politician and clean-shaven, to boot."

Mr. Biddle ignored the interruption, continuing: "The ceremony was followed by a splendid luncheon and then Charles—excuse me, your uncle—delivered a stirring ode honoring the memory of our Union dead before both Houses of the State Legislature."

"Most of the distinguished solons slept through it," Uncle Charles said acidly. "Not that I blame them. How did that verse begin?" He looked up at the ceiling for inspiration. "'Hail, you long-dead legions . . . marching now in memory's dust . . .' Something like that, anyway. Dear God, I was young then."

"I was shocked that your grandmother refused to attend," Mr. Biddle told me. He shook his head disbelievingly and the lines around his mouth looked like a parade of exclamation points.

Uncle Charles took a soothing sip of tea. "I wasn't," he said mildly. "She had already told me she would be ashamed to be seen in public with a man— and a relative at that—whose only work, as she put it, was rhyming words."

"Well, *I* was proud to be seen with you," Mr. Biddle said heatedly. "And I'm glad she wasn't there. She would have ruined the whole day with her everlasting judgments and disapprovals."

He paused for a moment and seemed to be looking at some memory deep inside of him. Then he smiled: "Do you remember, Charles, we stayed overnight at the Capitol Hotel, across the street from the Legislature, and dined there, in high fashion, on caviar and pheasant? There were candles on all the tables in the dining room and crisp white linen and we drank far too much champagne."

He stopped talking, then, and looked over at Uncle Charles and for the briefest moment his face changed as Uncle Charles's had earlier; the years fell away and I could see what he must have looked like as a young man. Uncle Charles looked quietly back at his friend and he, too, looked young again—for the same brief moment. And for some reason I couldn't quite understand I felt uncomfortable, as if I were an intruder in some private place.

But then the moment passed, and Uncle Charles, suddenly brisk, said, "Well, Andrew, Mr. Biddle and I have a lot to catch up on and it would be cruel to bore you with our more maudlin memories. And besides," he added, glancing out the window, "it's getting late—time for you to run along home before your charming father comes after you with a posse and a gun."

"Good-bye, Andrew," Mr. Biddle said as I slowly stood up, reluctant to say my good-byes to the sanctuary of Uncle Charles's rooms, to the stories of the past, and to the lessons in friendship I was learning. Mr. Biddle shook my hand again.

"It was a pleasure to meet another reader." He held my hand in his warm grip. "Don't YOU let your grandmother make you ashamed of loving books!"

I promised I wouldn't and said good-bye to him. I started to shake Uncle Charles's hand, too, but then, for some reason, I impulsively hugged him instead—the first time I had ever dared touch him. I felt his body stiffen with surprise but then he patted me awkwardly on the back and cleared his throat. "Run along now," he said.

And I did, galloping down the stairs but my mind was racing even faster, creating a fantastic vision of the future that I could not have imagined an hour before: a future in which I would no longer be alone but would have a friendship like Uncle Charles's and Mr. Biddle's! One that was built on trust and support and respect and common interests and mutual approval and memories as comfortable as the old leather chair Uncle Charles sat in to read.

It was twilight when I stepped out onto the porch. Deep shadows were spreading across the front lawn and covering the sidewalk and I realized that part of my picture of the future was similarly obscured: the part that would show me how to find such a friend.

I stepped off the porch to start up the hill toward home and shivered, suddenly. It was getting chilly but that wasn't the reason. It was because I sensed that someone was watching me. It felt like a pair of eyes had turned into knives that were stuck in my back. I looked up at the windows of Uncle Charles's rooms. He must have turned on a lamp after I left because warm yellow light was spilling out onto the roof but I didn't see either him or Mr. Biddle looking out. Instead, glancing down at the kitchen window, I saw Grandma's face pressed against the glass, staring intently at me. When she saw me turn around, she stepped back from the window but I felt her eyes continue to carve question marks in my back until I turned the corner out of her sight.

And then, shivering, I ran the rest of the way home.

• • •

Coming to visit Uncle Charles the following Saturday morning, I found Grandma waiting for me at the front door.

"Don't take your jacket off," she ordered. "We're going out."

"Where?" I asked.

"You'll see," was all she would say. And I knew better than to ask again.

Silently we got into her old black Chrysler and drove off through the leaf-strewn streets of town. It was fall still and the trees were bright splashes of color against a cloudless blue sky but for all the notice my grandmother took, she might as well have been living in a black-and-white movie, driving silently through town and then up the long hill past our church, its steeple so perfectly framed by the trees it seemed to shout, "Take a picture of me."

But Grandma ignored that, too, and we drove around the corner and pulled up, finally, in front of a shabby little house with peeling paint and a roof that sagged like the back of an old elephant.

"We're here," my grandmother announced, and my heart sank. "Here" was where Eddie Adams lived. The same Eddie Adams who was full of the devil and had made me cry at school.

My grandmother had driven me to hell.

I didn't even need to ask why, since she was telling me . . . briskly.

"I decided you needed some friends your own age, so I called Mrs. Adams and she was nice enough to invite you to come over and spend the afternoon with Eddie. Be sure to thank her."

"Grandma," I protested faintly, "Eddie Adams hates me."

"Don't be silly," my grandmother replied, biting off her words like an angry snapping turtle. "He doesn't hate you. He's a nice boy. He's in church every Sunday."

The only reason he was in church every Sunday was because his mother was the organist and made him go, but it would have been a waste of time to try to explain that to Grandma. Besides she was already out of the car and impatiently motioning me to join her. "Hurry up. It's not polite to keep them waiting."

We walked up the sidewalk, stepping over the weeds that grew through its cracks and climbed the three steps to the porch where my grandmother rapped briskly at the front door.

Mrs. Adams must have been waiting for us, since the door popped open immediately and she popped out after it like a cuckoo out of a clock. A big cuckoo—a *very* big cuckoo: She was about six feet tall but her hair—flaming red like Eddie's—was piled so high on top of her head that she looked as big as a small lighthouse.

Nobody in our town knew much about her but some people claimed she had once been an actress and I guess she did look pretty dramatic. Her makeup was so thick it could have been applied with a paint roller, and she was covered with jewelry—from the hoops in her ears to the rings circling every finger down to the ankle bracelets that made her legs look like a ring toss at the county fair.

"DEAR MRS. LOGAN," she boomed in a voice as deep as Uncle Charles's but twice as loud. And spreading her arms wide, she grabbed my grandmother and swept her into an enormous embrace. My mouth fell open. Hugging Grandma would be like hugging a stainless steel porcupine. Nobody did it. But Mrs. Adams sure did, squeezing away like an octopus with big red lips and false eyelashes. When she finally let Grandma go, she turned to me.

"AND HERE IS LITTLE ANDREW," she thundered, smiling at me like she was the big bad wolf and I was all three of the little pigs. At least she didn't hug me, but she did grab my hands and shake them like she was priming a pump. Then, holding them out in front of her, she gasped as if she had just had a vision of the baby Jesus, "ANDREW, THESE ARE THE HANDS OF A CON-CERT PIANIST."

These are the hands of an eleven-year-old fat boy, I thought, looking glumly down at my sausagelike fingers.

"DO YOU PLAY?"

"No, ma'am," I said.

"THEN YOU MUST HAVE LESSONS FROM ME!" She made it sound like the eleventh commandment. Thou shalt have no other piano teachers before me.

Grandma had gotten her breath back by now and was scowling at Mrs. Adams.

"And who's going to pay for them!" she demanded. "Not me, and his parents certainly don't have the money for such nonsense."

I think Mrs. Adams blushed —I know I did, but it was hard to tell under all that makeup. If she did, she sure recovered quickly.

"HAHAHAHA!" she boomed like the cemetery cannons on Decoration Day. "YOUR GRANDMOTHER IS A DELIGHT, ANDREW. SO OUTSPOKEN. I COULD JUST EAT HER UP."

Considering the size of her teeth, I figured she probably could but she'd have a terrible stomachache afterward.

"I thought your son was going to be here," Grandma said meaningfully.

"HE'S UPSTAIRS IN HIS ROOM," Mrs. Adams explained, "GETTING READY FOR LITTLE ANDREW'S VISIT. "

Yeah, I thought unhappily. Getting out all his knives and pitchforks.

Mrs. Adams leaned into the house. "EDWARD," she yodeled, "LITTLE ANDREW IS HERE."

Even outside on the front porch I could hear Eddie groan, "Oh, shit."

I groaned, too, but silently.

"RUN UPSTAIRS, ANDREW," Mrs. Adams urged. "DON'T KEEP HIM WAITING."

My grandmother, who always had to have the last word even when it made her the pot calling the kettle black, added: "Yes, don't be rude."

"Yes, ma'am," I said reluctantly and then saved myself from a scolding later by remembering to say to Mrs. Adams, "thank you very much for the invitation to come over."

Mrs. Adams showed me her teeth in a smile as insincere as my thank-you, and I went into the house.

I walked through the living room, noticing the battered upright piano in a corner and furniture so old and defeated-looking it must have come from the Salvation Army Thrift Shop. Eddie's family was even poorer than mine. No wonder Mrs. Adams wanted to give me piano lessons. Now that I was gone, she was probably trying to persuade my grandmother to take lessons herself. So she could be the life of the party. . . .

Feeling as worn out as the furniture, I trudged dutifully upstairs to Eddie's room where I found him lying on his bed reading a comic book. He ignored me but his brother, Evan, smiled and said, "Hi."

Evan was fourteen. His hair was unfashionably long and blonder than Eddie's—more like the color of copper. He was putting on a shirt that had a picture of a bird sewn on the pocket. On the back it said "Bird-of-Paradise Lounge and Restaurant." I knew that Mrs. Adams played the Hammond organ there at dinnertime and had gotten Evan a part-time job working in the kitchen. People at church talked about it, unhappy that their Sunday organist also played in a weeknight tavern.

I didn't know Evan very well, except from church.

When you're eleven years old, any boy three years older than you are is a god. Boys your own age are only demigods—or in the case of Eddie, demons.

Evan was a friendly god, though. "Hey, Andy," he said. "How's school?"

"He loves it," Eddie said darkly. "He's a brain." He put the comic book down and looked at me with an expression like he was seeing a bug. Not the interesting kind you study in science class but the kind that falls off the cafeteria ceiling into your lunch.

Evan grinned. "Then you should hang out with him more often, nimrod. Maybe some of his smarts'd rub off on you."

He rubbed his brother's head. Eddie scowled and, pulling away, muttered, "Go to hell."

"So what are you guys doing today?" Evan asked, ignoring his brother's bad temper. I guess he was used to it.

"We're goin' to the movies," Eddie said sourly. "Ma gave me five bucks."

"Wow." Evan whistled. "What bank did she rob?"

Eddie shrugged and ignored the question. "Too bad YOU have to work," he said, sounding smug and nasty at the same time.

Now it was Evan's turn to shrug. "It's a dirty job," he said cheerfully, "but somebody's got to do it." He grinned and winked at me.

I blushed.

"Have a good time," Evan said to me, ruffling my hair as he passed. "You, too, nimrod," he called at Eddie over his shoulder.

I heard him clatter down the stairs and I would have given anything, including my future, if it was him and not Eddie I was going to the movies with.

Eddie sighed as if someone had just told him the bus was leaving for the torture chamber.

"C'mon," he said to me. "Let's get this over with."

Eddie walked ahead of me on the way to the theater, obviously hoping no one would know we were together. He wasn't fooling anyone, though. His best friend, Billy Curtis—the same Billy who would bully me so mercilessly a year later—was standing outside the Isis Theater with a gang of guys from school.

"Hey, Adams," he yelled when he saw us. "Who's your date?"

"Shit; don't say anything," Eddie muttered to me. And, "Shut up," he yelled back at Billy, who made loud kissing noises.

Eddie blushed scarlet and looked like he might have a stroke. He threw his five-dollar bill at the woman in the ticket booth, grabbed the tickets and his change, and pushed me inside. We found seats and he sat, an empty seat between us, in sullen silence staring straight ahead while I industriously wished I were dead.

"I'm gonna get me some popcorn," Eddie said suddenly, getting up and pointedly not asking if I wanted anything.

I relaxed a little after he had gone and watched the coming attractions and the newsreel. I was surprised when he didn't come back for the cartoon. There must be an awful long line at the refreshment counter, I thought anxiously, since I knew he'd be mad if he missed the cartoon and would find some way to take it out on me. I wondered if I should take his place in line so he wouldn't miss any of the feature, too, but the theater was filling up and I was afraid that if I left our seats, someone else would take them and I'd be in even

worse trouble. So I stayed where I was and tried to concentrate on the show. It was a monster movie, a good
one with Lon Chaney, Jr., and despite myself I got so
absorbed that I actually forgot about Eddie. The monster was being pursued through a driving rainstorm by
a mob of torch-carrying peasants when I felt something
light hit my head and bounce off. I looked around curi-
ously but didn't see anything unusual so I turned back
to the screen. One of the peasants threw a rock, hitting
the monster and wounding it. The kids around me
cheered and something else hit me on the head. This
time I saw it bounce off: It was a kernel of popcorn. I
looked up and saw Eddie and Billy leaning over the
edge of the balcony above my head, grinning down at
me. Eddie reached into his bag and pulled out a handful of popcorn, which he sent showering down on my
upturned face. I looked away just as Billy upended his
Coke cup, sending its contents raining down on me like
a syrupy Niagara Falls, soaking my hair and shirt. A few
kids saw what happened and snickered but most were
too absorbed in the movie to notice. For even one kid
to see what had happened was more than I could bear,
though, and burning with shame, I crept out of the
auditorium just as another stone hit the monster; it
screamed and blood started to gush down its face.

I cleaned my glasses in the stale-urine-smelling
rest room, washed my hands and face, and tried to dry
my hair and clothes with paper towels, but it was hopeless. I was too wet—and too sticky. My skin crawled,
but that was nothing compared to the itch of humiliation I felt. I tried to hate Billy and Eddie for it but I realized that it was only myself I hated—for being the kind
of kid other boys tortured. And for being so weak I let
them get away with it.

I sighed and did the only thing I could do: I went back into the theater, stopping at the refreshment counter to buy a king-sized candy bar. I found a seat at the very back of the auditorium and stuffed the chocolate into my mouth while hot tears rolled over my fat cheeks.

The monster fell off a cliff finally, its body bouncing off rocks until, at the bottom, it fell into the sea and vanished beneath the waves.

The kids in the audience screamed approval and whistled piercingly as the words "The End" appeared on the screen and the houselights came up. I sat there in the last row by myself until everybody had left, hoping desperately that Billy and Eddie would have left, too. But, of course, they hadn't. They were loitering in the lobby as I knew they would be. After all, Eddie had missed the cartoon. He needed something to laugh at.

He grinned when he saw me. "Enjoy the movie, Logan?"

"Looks like he took a shower instead," Billy smirked, nudging Eddie in the ribs. "I guess fat people take showers in pop instead of water."

Then suddenly he scowled at me. "You owe me a Coke, fat boy; you made me spill my other one."

"Yeah," Eddie chimed in, "and you owe me a box of popcorn."

I couldn't believe what I was hearing. "I owe you a Coke and a box of popcorn," I repeated stupidly.

"Hey," Eddie said. "You're lucky I'm not making you pay me back for your ticket."

"But you invited me," I protested weakly.

Eddie looked at Billy and then back at me. "Man, for someone who's supposed to be so smart, you're really stupid, you know that? The only reason I took you to the movies was because your grandmother paid my mother to make me go with you."

Eddie laughed. "I mean, why else would anybody go with you?"

His words were sharp rocks hitting me.

"No shit," Billy hooted. "Old Lady Logan actually paid your mother?"

"Yeah," Eddie said. "Can you believe it?"

Then he turned on me, pressing his face so close to mine I could see the pores scattered among the freckles on his skin. He grabbed a roll of fat at my waist, his fingers digging into the soft flesh. "But if you tell anybody I told you, I'll beat the shit out of you, understand?"

Boys are like dogs. They know when you're afraid of them. And that knowledge brings out the killer in them. And, of course, I *was* afraid of these two. And that was worse than anything else that had happened to me because the fear would always be part of me. It was the tool they could always use to fix me good.

"I understand," I whispered. And I went to the refreshment stand and bought them a giant Coke and a jumbo popcorn.

• • •

"What happened to you," my grandmother demanded when she picked me up later. I had dutifully walked back to the Andrews house with Billy and Eddie close behind me, whispering together, taking turns stepping on my heels, and laughing.

"I spilled a Coke on myself in the movie," I mumbled.

My grandmother sighed one of her can't-you-do-anything-right sighs. "Well, be sure your mother washes those clothes the minute you get home. Otherwise they'll be permanently stained."

"Yes, ma'am," I mumbled.

"Well, anyway. Aside from that, did you have a good time?"

"I guess," I lied.

"See," my grandmother replied as if I had just yelled whoopee and done cartwheels on the front seat of the car. "I knew you'd have a good time with someone your own age. Maybe you can go out with him again next week."

And she smiled the serenely satisfied smile of one who always knows best.

• • •

I told Uncle Charles what had happened. I poured my heart out to him, in fact, telling him far more than I had intended. And then, of course, I had to cry—stupid, stormy sobs.

"Oh, dear God," Uncle Charles said nervously. "Don't cry, Andrew. Please. Words I can deal with. But tears are impossible."

"I'm sorry," I sniffed, wiping my eyes on the back of my hand and trying to push my tears back inside. "I can't help it. It hurts too bad not to cry."

"*Plus c'est change . . .*" Uncle Charles murmured. "The more things change . . ." He sank back in his chair and sat quietly for a moment, looking old and tired.

"Of course, it hurts," he said. "Believe me, Andrew, I know. From painful firsthand experience. I was bait for the bullies, too, when I was your age."

He gave me a sad smile and patted my hand awkwardly. "Does that surprise you? It shouldn't. Look at me: You may be the largest boy in your class but I was always the smallest in mine and the brightest, too—just like you. It's a deadly combination, isn't it: to be physically AND mentally different from all the others?"

"Why can't they just leave me alone?" I demanded resentfully, trying to fight back a flood of new tears. "I'm not hurting anybody."

Uncle Charles frowned thoughtfully. "Well . . . maybe at some deep level they feel you are. Children are herd animals, after all, and are afraid of anything they don't understand. So they instinctively turn their fear of the unknown into self-righteous anger. That way they can feel justified, even virtuous, in destroying anything that threatens the survival of the herd by being different. Adults are the same way. Your grandmother may say she wants you to find "friends your own age." But what she really wants is for you to find acceptance by becoming a faceless part of the herd."

He shook his head in disapproval.

"I don't think that's what you want, Andrew. At least I hope it isn't, although I admit it's terribly hard to be different because it invites the too-easy belief that something is wrong with you. Believe me, the hardest lesson I ever had to learn in my life was to welcome my differences—to value them. I hope you'll learn that lesson, too."

Part of me knew he was right but his cool-sounding logic and good sense brought no comfort at all to my still-hurting heart. What he called "valuing my differences" seemed to promise only a lifetime of solitude. Of always standing apart, of always being alone, and of never realizing the beautiful but rapidly fading dream of friendship I had had only a week before.

"It's not fair," I burst out. "I'm lonesome. You're lucky; you've got Mr. Biddle but I don't have anybody."

Uncle Charles raised an eyebrow. "I'm afraid your grandmother doesn't think I'm lucky; she never did approve of my friendship with Horace."

"Why not?" I persisted.

"Because of what I told you a moment ago," he answered patiently; "she doesn't understand it and so she's afraid of it. Look, Andrew, sometimes friendship is not something you understand here"—he pointed to his head; "sometimes it's something you can only comprehend here"—and this time he pointed to his heart. "Do you see?"

"No," he said, looking at my blank expression; "I see you don't."

There was an awkward silence. He drummed his fingers on the arm of his chair and then suddenly turned to the nearest shelf and reached for a book, which he handed to me.

"This book has some exceedingly interesting things to say about friendship, Andrew. It's not easy reading but I think you can understand most of it. Give it a try, anyway; perhaps it will help."

I glanced at the spine and brightened. "It's by C.S. Lewis," I said eagerly. "He wrote the Narnia books."

"So he did," Uncle Charles said. "I had forgotten. Well, you'll find this one somewhat different, I'm afraid, but come to think of it, friendship does have some of Narnia's magic.

"No, don't read it here," he said, as I eagerly started to open the book. "Take it home where you can be alone and concentrate. After you've read it, perhaps we can talk about it."

• • •

I started to read the book that same evening after my parents had gone to bed. Uncle Charles was right; it *was* different from the Narnia books and I didn't understand all of it. Fortunately he had underlined the most important parts and some of *those* sounded familiar.

For example: "Friendship is essentially between individuals," I read, "the moment two men are friends they have in some degree drawn apart together from the herd . . . The pack or herd may even dislike and distrust friendship."

Remembering what Uncle Charles had tried to explain, I understood something else I read about friendship: "It is a relation between two men at their highest level of individuality."

That ought to be enough to scare the herd into stampeding right off the nearest cliff, I thought with a grin and read on. I didn't finish the book that night. Or the next. Because it wasn't like reading a story. I had to stop and think about what I was reading. And a lot of the time I found myself thinking about Uncle Charles and Mr. Biddle. Particularly when the author said friendship has to be about something "the others do not share and which, till that moment, each believed to be his own unique treasure or burden."

I thought about the treasure of Uncle Charles's books and the burden of books Mr. Biddle had been carrying the first time I saw him and I thought about the books *I* had shared with Uncle Charles and suddenly I realized how wrong Grandma had been when she said it was unnatural for me to spend so much time with "that old man." Now it seemed like the most natural thing in the world. And the most natural thing in the world for those *two* old men to have been friends all these years.

One thing about the book bothered me, though: its title, *The Four Loves*. I had never thought of friendship as being love; I thought about Eddie and Billy; about how everybody said they were best friends but how could they be if friendship was a kind of love? Even

worse, Lewis said, "It is the sort of love one can imagine between angels." Billy and Eddie were sure no
angels.

I needed to ask Uncle Charles about these things
but I never got the chance.

He died before I could—somewhere in the middle
of a long winter night less than a month after he loaned
me the book. He had been ill with a cold for several
weeks and the doctor, afraid it might develop into
pneumonia, had ordered him to bed. My grandmother
grudgingly brought his meals to him on a tray. Taking
his breakfast to him one frosty morning, she found him
dead in bed, propped up against the pillows, a book
lying open on his chest as if he had placed it there for
just a moment to rest his eyes.

When my mother told me Uncle Charles had died,
I made a noise that sounded like a strangled laugh. It
was the sound of disbelief. How could he have died?
How could my only friend have left me without even
saying good-bye?

"He died peacefully in his sleep," Mother said
reassuringly. "What a wonderful way to die."

No death is wonderful when it takes away your
only friend, I wanted to shout at her. Instead I made
some more strangled noises, but now they were sobs. I
was crying and couldn't stop. My mother's face was
pinched with anxiety as she watched me cry.

"He was an old man, Andy," she said. "He lived a
long time. He had a good life."

"He wasn't an old man," I sobbed. "He was my
friend. "

"I know he was," my mother soothed, "but crying
like this isn't going to bring him back. It'll just make
you sick."

"Good," I said, "then I can die, too, and be with him."

Now my mother looked shocked. "Andy, don't talk like that. It's tempting God."

And then her face changed and she looked cunning. "Your Uncle Charles wouldn't want you crying like this for him."

She was right. He wouldn't have known how to deal with the tears. But it wasn't him I was crying for. It was me. And not just because I had lost my friend. I had lost something else, too. Uncle Charles's rooms hadn't been Ali Baba's cave, after all. They had been something infinitely better: They had been home. And now my home was gone. And where on earth could I go to find another sanctuary so welcoming? And what would become of me?

•   •   •

Mr. Biddle came to the funeral home in a taxi. The cab driver pushed him, in a wheelchair, into the deserted room where Uncle Charles lay in his casket for what the funeral director called "visitation." The driver stood at the door, looking on uncomfortably while Mr. Biddle wheeled himself slowly through the empty room toward me.

"Hello, Andrew," he said. His voice sounded like dust, whispering through the air. I was almost afraid to shake the hand he offered me because he looked so frail I thought it might crumble into dust, too, if I so much as touched it.

"Push me closer, please," he said.

I pushed the wheelchair right up next to the coffin. Mr. Biddle stared at Uncle Charles for a long time. And then he said to me, "Help me up, Andrew." He was so light I think I could have lifted him up with one hand. His body seemed almost like a shadow of a real body

that existed now only in the past—like a dead language.
Once out of his wheelchair, he leaned against the casket
to steady himself. And then he touched Uncle Charles's
cheek so gently with the back of his hand that it was as
if a single snowflake had landed there. And slowly and
painfully, he bent over and pressed his lips to Uncle
Charles's forehead. It wasn't really like a kiss at all. It
was more like his lips were two flower petals being
pressed in the pages of a book—for remembrance.

"Good-bye, old friend," he whispered. "*Requiescat
in pace.*"

And then, "Thank you, Andrew," he sighed. "I'm
ready to go now."

I helped him sit back down and then I pushed him
to the door. The taxi driver took over from there. And
pushed Mr. Biddle out of the room and away into the
winter night.

When they were gone, I cried again. But not for me
this time. Or for Uncle Charles. But for Mr. Biddle. I think
he was so old and so dried out inside that he couldn't
have done it for himself. And I knew he wanted to.

·　·　·

Uncle Charles's was the first funeral I had ever
gone to and it was a grave disappointment. I guess I
expected it to be held in a big cathedral with a ceiling
as high as heaven and windows of stained glass as full
of colors as the spines of his books.

But Uncle Charles didn't belong to any church and
so his funeral was held in the Hofmeister Funeral Home
on River Street. Presiding was Mr. Hofmeister himself, a
heavyset, jowly man in a business suit and clip-on
necktie. His voice sounded like the man on the inter-
com who calls the attention of shoppers to the latest
bargain. Admitting that he had never known Uncle

Charles (or "Brother Abbott" as he called him), the man proceeded to list a series of generic attributes that would have had Uncle Charles cocking an askance eyebrow. The words "book" and "mind" were never mentioned, presumably because they were not in Mr. Hofmeister's double-knit vocabulary. The service itself took place in a side room that looked like a page from a Formica catalog. Mrs. Hofmeister sang "Nearer My God to Thee" in a wobbly soprano while playing a Hammond chord organ. The only thing that saved the day for me was the graveside service. It turned out that Uncle Charles was not to be buried, like a normal person. Instead, his casket was to be placed in a vault in the wall of a mausoleum.

"Geezus," my father whispered to my mother in a voice that could have been heard in the next county, "this gives me the creeps."

Way to go, Uncle Charles, I thought, valuing this last of his differences.

●　●　●

The next day my father commandeered me to help carry some of the funeral flowers to my grandmother's. Not yet as dead as Uncle Charles but well on their way, the flowers turned the frosty air almost sultry with fragrant decay. It had warmed up enough the day before to rain (Why does it always rain on the day of a funeral, my mother had sighed) but the temperature had dropped overnight and there had been a hard freeze. The trees were sheathed in ice and the mud puddles in the alley we followed to Grandma's were also covered by a skiff of ice. It would melt soon, though. The sun had come out and it was already warming up enough to turn the unpaved alley muddy. Between carrying the flowers, which obscured my vision, and looking down at my feet to avoid the puddles, I didn't see what made my father stop short and say, "Geezus! What the hell is she doing?"

I lowered the flowers and looked up. We had come within sight of the house and I could see Grandma's figure appear at one of the windows of Uncle Charles's second-story rooms. Her arms were full of something, some burden which, as I watched with the kind of frozen fascination that a mouse watches a snake, she heaved out.

The armload of books fell through the smoky winter air, their pages fluttering like the broken wings of pale birds, and landed with a series of sickening thuds in the alley. Some of them fell in the puddles, breaking through the thin layer of ice and sending up splashes of dirty water. Without pausing for breath my industrious grandmother gathered up another armload of books.

"Stop!" I screamed without even knowing I was going to say it. "Stop!" I was suddenly running down the alley, so frantic in my haste that water from the flower vases sloshed out onto my jacket and pants. I didn't even notice. "Stop!" I shouted a third time, stopping directly under the window.

My grandmother looked down at me in open-mouthed astonishment.

"You can't do that," I said, breathing hard from the exertion of running but also from the fear I felt of defying her. "Those are Uncle Charles's books."

If my grandmother had been taken aback by my act of defiance, she regained her composure immediately.

"They're my books now," she told me grimly, "and I can do anything I want with them." And as if to prove it, she dropped another armload out the window to fall heavily, lifelessly, in the mud at my feet.

My clothes were wet, but the water on my face was not from the flower vases; it was from the tears streaming down my cheeks as I turned desperately to my father who was now standing beside me. "Make her stop," I pleaded. "Please make her stop."

"Geezus, Ma," the old man said, ignoring me. "What are ya doin'?"

"What does it look like I'm doing?" she demanded. "I'm getting rid of these damn books. I can't rent his rooms with these books cluttering them up."

"But they're valuable," I pleaded. "You can't just throw them away."

"They're worthless to me," my grandmother said stubbornly.

"But Uncle Charles," I started to protest.

"You shut up!" my grandmother snapped. "I've taken about enough lip from you, young man. Your precious Uncle Charles was worthless, too. And if you're not careful, you're going to turn out to be just like him."

She stared angrily down at me, breathing as hard as I was, as if the words she had thrown down at me were as heavy as the books. She hates me, I thought in amazement. My own grandmother hates me.

"And what's the matter with you," she scowled at my father. "Can't you control your own son? Are you going to let him get away with talking to me like that?"

"Don't argue with your grandma," my father said. But without conviction and without even looking at me. As if it was something he didn't really believe but had to say anyway.

"I'm sorry, Ma," he called up to his mother. "But the kid's right about one thing. These books *are* valuable. We could sell 'em."

"Well, then, get your lazy butt up here and box

them up," my grandmother snapped at him. "I can't do it all by myself. I don't have time. There's too much other work to be done, getting these rooms ready to rent. As for you," she scowled down at me, "you pick those books up off the ground and put them in the trash."

Then, with the assurance of a field commander who knows his orders will be unquestioningly obeyed, she stepped back from the window and slammed it shut so viciously it was a miracle the glass didn't shatter.

"Do what she says," my father told me. Only he didn't sound like my father anymore. He sounded like a little boy who was as scared of his mother as I was of him. My angry, red-faced, raging father sounded . . . meek and so ashamed I felt as if I were doing him a favor by not looking at him.

"Yessir," I mumbled, looking down at the mud beneath my feet instead.

When he had gone inside, I started picking up books. They were a mess—covered with mud, spines broken, pages torn. I tried to wipe away as much mud as possible—on my jacket and trousers—and to smooth out wrinkled pages. But it was hopeless. All I could really do was stack them neatly next to the trash cans—to give them a decent burial, I thought sadly. At least the rest of the books still upstairs would be saved. Maybe. I could hear my grandmother yelling at my father in the house, and I was glad I couldn't hear what she was saying.

Miraculously one book had landed on its back, so its spine was unbroken, and since it had fallen on a narrow strip of dead grass that separated the house from the alley, it was clean, though wet. I picked it up and dried it off on my jacket. It was an old book and had been handled so often that the once-gilt letters of the author's name had been rubbed off the spine. I opened the book to its title page and read: *Pensées,* by Blaise Pascal. There was something else on the title page: an inscription written in a flowery, old-fashioned handwriting: "To Charles Augustus Abbott, The Friend of My Heart." It was signed "Horace Biddle" and dated fifty years earlier. Underneath the inscription Uncle Charles had written a page number. I turned to it and found a passage underlined. My heart beat faster as I read the words, "The heart has its reasons which the mind cannot know."

I closed the book. And immediately reopened it. There was something I had to do. I pulled two petals off a flower in one of the vases I had carried and closed them in the book at the underlined page. For remembrance. By dying, Uncle Charles had become part of my past. But this book, which had belonged to him and had been important to him and which I could read whenever I wanted, could make him part of my present, too. And so I carefully slipped the book up under my shirt where it would be safe and hidden from my grandmother and my father. I wondered how much Uncle Charles had had to keep hidden and I understood that, to survive—and in an odd sort of way, for him to survive with me—I would have to keep much hidden, too—as I already hid my reading from my father—until I was old enough for my heart to find its own reasons. Meanwhile the book that rested secretly against my body would help.

I remembered what Uncle Charles had said about valuing my differences. I believed now that it was good to be different from Eddie and Billy—and from my father and grandmother. I also found comfort in the fact I wasn't different from everybody, certainly not from Uncle Charles and Mr. Biddle. And feeling the comforting weight of the book against my body, I could even believe that someday I might find somebody else who valued my differences. With whom I could be myself, whoever that turned out to be. And maybe, if I were lucky, that person would be someone whom I could call a friend of *my* heart.

I smiled at the thought and hugged the book to my chest.

Ave, Uncle Charles, I whispered. *Requiescat in pace.*

Andy in Love

Andy in Love

After a while, hiding important things like the way you feel becomes such an ingrained habit of survival that it turns into second nature. It's like a chameleon's changing color to blend into its background. You do it so automatically you don't even know you've done it and as a result, you wind up hiding emotions not only from other people but from yourself, too.

That's why I got so mad when Stevenson made his crack about my having a crush on Professor Hawthorne. It scared me that feelings I wasn't even aware of might be so obvious to someone else.

Do I have a crush on him? I ask myself.

The answer is, I don't know. I only know that of all my teachers, his is the only biography I have looked up in the library. And maybe something *is* going on in my hidden heart because the whole time I was reading *Who's Who* I was afraid someone would discover me at it, as if it was something to be ashamed of. As if it turned me into an eighth-grade girl with a crush on a movie star.

Or a TV star?

I stretch. The overhead lights blink and I look at my watch. I'm surprised to see it's already five o'clock and I remember the library closes early on Homecoming day. It's time for me to go back to the dorm.

I grab a couple of books for company, knowing I'll be alone tonight like every night. At the checkout desk I recognize the librarian, a nice woman who looks like my mother. As she stamps my books, she asks, "Don't you ever take a day off?"

I mumble something that sounds like "No-ma'am-I-guess-not-thanks" and, tucking the books under my arm, I start back for the dorm. The sun is making a big show of setting, commanding a few scattered clouds to appear so it can make them look like they're marshmallows on fire. Everything is so beautiful I wonder why I'm so goddam depressed. The campus is deserted now in the twilight. I know everybody is rushing manically around in the dorms and the frat and sorority houses—laughing, shouting at each other, getting ready to head off to big-deal parties, but I have this crazy idea that, instead, they're all hiding somewhere so they don't have to be around me. Who cares, I think. I don't need *them*. What I do need is my run but, perversely, I don't go to the track. Instead I go to the Arena, a pizza place a block off campus, and order a pizza to go. While I wait for my order, I sit in a booth by the window and watch the people sitting at the counter—a sad-faced woman and an old guy wearing a hat and sipping coffee. They look as depressed as I am. My pizza's ready, finally, and I carry it back to the dorm. It's dark outside now and really cold. I dive into the pizza when I get to my room, stuffing piece after piece into my mouth, hoping that if I pig out, I'll feel better.

But I don't. I'm miserably full when I finish but there's still room inside for some self-hating guilt because I skipped my run. I lie down on the bed and open one of the books, a collection of sermons by Jonathan Edwards, this eighteenth-century minister

Professor Hawthorne has been raving about. I read one of his really cheerful sermons called "Sinners in the Hands of an Angry God" and I fall asleep with the lights on thinking of my old man.

● ● ●

I wake up early the next morning, still feeling guilty as hell because I didn't do my run the day before—or maybe because it's Sunday and I don't go to church anymore. I lie in bed, half-asleep and half-awake, drowsily thinking about my mother, knowing she's already up at home, getting ready to head off to her adult Bible class and an hour of church. And then because my mind is so predictable, I think of Evan and those thoughts drive me out of bed and into my sweats. I head down the hall, hearing someone throwing up in the bathroom. Party hearty, pal, I think. The rosy sun is just coming up as I hit the track and run and run and run and think and think and think—about my church, my church, my dear old church, and about Evan who might have been mine, too. . . .

Like Angel Wings, Part 1

Like Angel Wings, Part 1

"Thank God for my faith," Mother said fervently. And sighed.

I used to imagine that if you could somehow collect those sighs, within a week—if you were lucky—you'd have enough wind for a gale force strong enough to blow my father out to sea, where he could sleep with the fishes instead of passed out in his underwear on the living room sofa.

It was a sweet-smelling Sunday morning. Though Easter was still six weeks away, spring had already arrived. Flowers were blooming everywhere and trees were covered with buds. Mother and I were headed for church in the family car, which I called the Dentmobile, because it looked like it had been driven in a demolition derby. In a sense I guess it had, since my father, the well-known drunk driver, was usually behind the wheel. But this morning it was Mother who was doing the driving. The sun was shining down on us like a big smile in the sky, and the old man was just a bad memory of the night before when he had come home drunk as usual and thrown up on the rag rug outside the bathroom.

"Oh, Hal," Mother had sighed wearily. "I just washed that rug."

"Well, excuse me all to hell," the old man muttered, adding thickly, "I feel like shit."

You look like it, too, I thought as I headed for the utility room to get a mop and bucket to clean up his sour-smelling mess. Meanwhile my mother was busy cleaning up *her* sour-smelling mess and putting him to bed like a helpless, red-faced baby with whiskey breath.

"Why don't you divorce him?" I demanded the next morning. "I'm tired of cleaning up his messes."

"Oh, Andy," was her answer. "You know why. When I married him, it was for better or worse."

"Be sure to tell me when we get to better," I said shortly and immediately felt guilty because I knew she truly believed what she said.

"Don't always be so sarcastic," Mother said and looked away.

Thanks to God and my mother's faith in Him, we spent two stuffy hours in worship every Sunday: one hour in Sunday School and one in church. But I didn't mind . . . too much. After all, it was two hours of my week away from the old man, who wouldn't set foot inside a church. Come to think of it, maybe that's why Mother liked going there, too.

We turned a corner and the church came into view, the cross atop its steeple seeming to float there like a promise.

"Promise me," Mother said, trying to maneuver into a too-small parking place, "that you'll never be a drinker like your father."

"*Mother*," I protested.

"No," she said, "I mean it. His drinking is my cross to bear but I don't think I *could* bear it if you turned out like him."

Now it was my turn to sigh. "I promise."

"Thank you, dear," my mother said, "you're a good son."

You bet, Mom, I thought, I'm the best little son in the whole, wide world. Everybody says so. The little old ladies at church love me, patting my cheek and cooing over me. So polite. So thoughtful. So . . . *good*.

Of course I was good. I was afraid not to be. I was afraid to be discourteous. Afraid to be thoughtless. Afraid to be . . . *me*, whoever that was. For if my mother found the comfort of blessed assurance in her religion, all I found was the promise of retribution in mine.

"FOR I, THE LORD YOUR GOD, AM A JEALOUS GOD," Pastor Peterson thundered, pounding the pulpit Sunday after Sunday, "VISITING THE INIQUITY OF THE FATHERS UPON THE CHILDREN UNTO THE THIRD AND FOURTH GENERATION OF THEM THAT HATE ME.

"And showing mercy unto thousands of them that love me," he added softly, like a secret loophole he didn't want to share with the congregation.

Well, gee, I thought, that's great, but it's not going to do little me a whole lot of good, is it, since I found it hard to love a God whom I saw in my mind's eye as my father—but holding a flaming sword instead of the usual fifth of Scotch.

Pastor Peterson wasn't real big on love, either. He preferred to talk about something he called "muscular Christianity." And his favorite hymn was "Onward, Christian Soldiers." And his favorite sermon topic was Jesus' getting hot under the collar and chasing the moneylenders out of the temple. Evan Adams called it his "Jesus kicks butt" sermon and made us kids laugh. Except when his mother was around. She was still our church organist, even though she looked more than ever like the Queen of the Gypsies.

As for me: I was a freshman in high school now, which meant that Evan was a senior. Since his younger brother Eddie hadn't robbed a bank or murdered anyone . . . *yet*—he was still around, too. Not that I saw much of him. He had his own friends. And I had . . . the old ladies at church.

"Hurry now," Mother urged, "or we'll be late for Sunday school."

I relaxed. Talk about blessed assurance. That's what she said every Sunday. God's in his heaven; we're going to be late for Sunday school. And every Sunday we were among the first to arrive. Getting out of the car, we hustled across the street and around the corner to the parish hall, an attached building that housed the Sunday school. This particular Sunday we were so early that Pastor Peterson himself was still standing outside, smoking a cigarette.

Wearing a black suit and clerical collar, he looked more like a Catholic priest than a Protestant minister, but I think he liked the outfit because it resembled a uniform, and he had been a chaplain in the Marine Corps. Six feet two inches tall, with a face like a clenched fist and a crew cut the color and texture of shredded wheat, he had big hands that could hurt you. Evan called him "Old Leatherlung" instead of "Old Leatherneck," though, because it wasn't those hands he used to bludgeon the congregation into submission, it was his voice; it exploded like mortar shells in the sanctuary.

Incoming, I thought, as he opened his mouth now.

"GOOD MORNING," he bellowed, as if Mother and I were slightly deaf and standing a block away.

"Good morning, Pastor," Mother whispered, looking down, as always, as if she had confused the pastor with God and was afraid to look upon his face.

"Morning there, Andy boy," he said to me. I shook his extended hand. He crunched mine in return. Muscular Christianity stuff. It hurt.

"Beautiful morning to worship God," he said sternly as if expecting an argument from us.

"Every morning is a beautiful morning to worship God," my mother said. And the pastor looked put out, as if she had just stolen his punch line. And perhaps she had.

We were saved from an awkward silence by the fluttering arrival of two more members of Pastor Peterson's flock: Thelma and Velma Thornton, two identical sisters in their eighties. They lived together, dressed alike in ruffles and flounces, and finished each other's sentences. No one could tell them apart. I'm not sure they could either after all those years of living together.

"Good," one of them said.

"Morning," the other one finished.

"GOOD MORNING, LADIES," Pastor Peterson thundered. The old women's hands flew up to their hearing aids and, seeing that the pastor was momentarily distracted, we gladly mumbled hasty good-byes and slipped inside.

You entered the parish hall on a landing between floors. Upstairs were the library and the Sunday school rooms. Downstairs was a reception room and beyond that a kitchen and a big open room with a tile floor where folding chairs were set up for the short devotional service that preceded Sunday school.

Mrs. Peterson, the pastor's wife, was standing at the foot of the steps. Plump as a partridge, she was a little woman who always wore her honey-colored hair in a braid wrapped around her head. Her eyes were a powder blue so pale they looked like a frozen lake at the top of the world. But don't think she was a cold person; in fact, she was warm and friendly and I liked her a lot. All the kids did. As a kind of affectionate shorthand we called her "Mrs. P."

"Hello, Emily," Mother greeted her. "I was sorry to hear about Benjie."

Benjie was the Petersons' eight-year-old son. He was a skinny little kid with curly hair and asthma. He'd had a bad attack on Saturday and had been rushed to the hospital.

"He's doing much better," Mrs. P. said reassuringly. "But thanks for your concern." She looked over at me as if to change the subject.

"Hello, Andy," she said, patting my arm, "you're looking very handsome today."

"He's too thin," Mother fussed. "It's all that running he does."

Mrs. P. winked at me. "Oh, I don't know," she said. "You can never be too rich or too thin. At least that's what they tell me, I wouldn't know from personal experience." She patted her stomach and laughed.

I smiled sympathetically. For my part, I couldn't imagine being too rich or too thin, but I sure could imagine being too fat. I had been and, in my mind at least, I always would be.

Mrs. P. and Mother started talking about church stuff, so I excused myself and went inside and looked around. A small crowd of sleepy-eyed adults and noisy kids was already assembling. A lectern had been set up at the front of the room next to an old upright piano. Seated on the bench in front of it was my idol of the moment: Evan Adams, who played for the devotional service. His mother had taught him to play both the piano and organ, but I suspected he could have played like a professional musician without a single lesson if he had wanted to. He was that kind of kid—a natural at anything he tried, whether it was hitting piano keys or a baseball, though that wasn't his sport. Gymnastics was. I'd never seen anyone as comfortable with his body as Evan. Most kids—like me—were klutzes. I could trip over my feet while standing still. But Evan did everything with such easy grace it was a pleasure to watch him breathe. He was like a beautiful present God had given the world. And, as usual, a group of girls were hanging around him, looking as if they'd like to unwrap him.

Evan was paying as much attention to them as a light does to the moths circling it. Instead he was thumbing through a hymnal, looking for an opening piece to play. He found one, marked the place, and put the book on the music rack. Then he seemed to notice the girls for the first time. He grinned at them, said something, and they all giggled hysterically.

"At ease, girls," Mr. Shelton said. Only, "girls" came out sounding something like "guh-wells."

Mr. Shelton was our Sunday school superinten-dent. His first name was Stanley but all the kids (and some of the crueler adults) called him "Elmer" because he had a speech impediment and sounded just like the cartoon character Elmer Fudd. He always carried a handkerchief in his right hand because public speaking made him nervous and sweaty. I don't know why, though, because nobody ever listened to him. He mopped his brow and said, "C'mon, girls, find your seats." His voice had taken on a slightly pleading tone. He was the kind of man who never ordered or even asked. Instead, he begged. Maybe that's why, as usual, the girls ignored him and continued giggling and talking and batting their eyes at Evan.

"All right, girls," *Mrs.* Shelton snapped. "That's enough nonsense. Find your seats this instant."

A head taller than her husband, Marie Shelton was a thin, angular woman with features so sharp she looked like an ax with lips. And because she had a tongue to match, she was accustomed to being obeyed. The girls didn't disappoint her, scattering to their seats as if they were a flock of turkeys and she was a farmer the day before Thanksgiving.

The devotions and the Sunday school hour that followed proceeded with comfortable predictability. Even the awful Eddie's absence from class was predictable, since his mother was out of town playing the organ for the opening of a new shopping mall somewhere and he had taken the opportunity to skip both Sunday school *and* church. Evan wasn't in class, either, not because he had skipped but because he would have to play the church organ in his mother's absence; in fact, we could hear faint snatches of the music he was practicing next door in the sanctuary. At one point Mrs. P., who taught the class I was in, held up her hand for silence and we listened to a passage so elaborate it sounded like sculpture being turned into music.

Mrs. P. shook her head in wonder. "That boy plays like an angel," she said softly.

"He looks like one, too," one of the girls said; the other girls giggled and fanned themselves, and Mrs. P. pretended she hadn't noticed.

The church service went as usual, too. Pastor Peterson preached about Jesus' restoring sight to the blind beggar nigh unto Jericho and thundered that all of us had been blinded by sin and that if we weren't careful, when the scales finally dropped from our eyes, we would see that *we* had landed in hell.

"I thought we were there already," I whispered to my mother.

"Hush," she said sharply out of the corner of her mouth.

The worship service ended with announcements, or—since they were coming from the pastor—*pronouncements*. He reminded us that the following Wednesday would be Ash Wednesday, the beginning of the Lenten season.

"I invite all of you to join us for services beginning at seven-thirty," he boomed. "But now it's time to adjourn to the parish hall for a half hour of Sunday fellowship. Or as I like to call it, heh-heh, our Christian kaffee klatsch."

That was supposed to be a joke and everybody chuckled dutifully, although I think most people, wanting to get home and take a nap or read the funnies, liked to call it a pain in the butt, instead.

Of course, *we* stayed for the fellowship hour. And in fact, since Pastor Peterson's "invitation" was more like an order, most of the other parishioners trooped over to the parish hall, too, and drank lukewarm instant coffee and ate stale gingersnaps. Pulling chairs together in little circles, the women sat and gossiped while the men smoked cigarettes, fanned themselves with wrinkled copies of the church bulletin, and talked about sports. I hung out next to a plastic flower-filled planter in one of the far corners of the room and practiced being invisible.

I did a lousy job of it, though, since Patti Shelton saw me right away and came over.

"Hi, Andy," she said in her soft, flat voice.

Patti, Mr. and Mrs. Shelton's daughter, was my age and I'd known her all my life. But it's still hard for me to describe her because unless I was looking at her, I forgot what she looked like. I always thought of her as the "kind of kid" because everything about her—except her big, round glasses, which fogged up when she got excited—was "kind of." I mean, she had kind of mouse-colored hair, kind of brown eyes, and kind of bad skin; her teeth were kind of crooked and she was kind of fat and kind of short. She was just totally nondescript like her father. I suspected that she knew it, too.

Maybe that's why, when she turned fourteen, she started spelling her name with an "i" instead of a "y." I guess she thought it would make her seem different or exotic. But I thought it just made her seem stupid. So I called her "Patti-with-an-i." Put a face and a body on one of my mother's sighs and you'd have Patti Shelton. I knew I was being mean and I felt guilty about it, but when you're a kicked-around kid like me, I guess you take it out on other people. What a great world.

"You look nice today," she told me, "huh-huh-huh." Patti-with-an-i didn't have a speech impediment like her father but she did have a habit of finishing every sentence with a little forced laugh that made her sound embarrassed as hell.

"You, too," I mumbled, looking around the room for someone to rescue me. Mercifully I caught Evan's eye. Surrounded by a group of little old ladies who were pinching his cheek and telling him what a wonderful organist he was, he looked like he needed rescuing, too. Sure enough, when he caught my eye, he gladly excused himself from his cooing flock and came over to stand between Patti and me.

"Hi, guys," he said, putting an arm around our

shoulders and giving each of us a one-armed hug.

I thought Patti was going to faint and I felt kind of weak in the knees myself, because Evan was the kind of older kid you worshipped. Most seniors made freshmen feel like pimples on a pig's butt, but Evan made you feel like a human being; he actually listened to you when you talked. The bad part about that was it sometimes made me tongue-tied, because I was afraid he'd think anything *I* might have to say was stupid.

That didn't stop Patti, though. After a "Hi, Evan, you look nice today, huh-huh-huh," she launched into a long, incredibly boring story about how her mother was teaching her to sew and how she was going to make her own dress for Easter.

I don't know how he did it, but polite Evan managed to look as rapt as if he were listening to Scheherazade. I guess he forgot that might encourage Patti to go on talking for a thousand nights and a night, but fortunately—before that could happen—her father came shambling over, his feet slapping the floor as if he were wearing big clown shoes.

"Your mother wants to see you, Patti," he said.

Patti looked put out.

"Now," Mr. Shelton said.

And Patti, who knew better than to keep *her* mother waiting, reluctantly said "good-bye, huh-huh-huh," and walked off.

I expected Mr. Shelton to follow—I don't think his wife ever let him out of her sight for more than two minutes—but instead he stuck around, clearing his throat and nervously lighting a cigarette, looking like he was smoking about six at once.

"Well," he said at last, "what are you wascals up to?"

"Oh, just tryin' to stay out of trouble," Evan said pleasantly.

"That's good," Mr. Shelton said and, wiping his forehead on the back of his sleeve, spilled ashes on his shoes.

"That's good," he repeated. "You don't want to get into twouble in church."

There was a gaping hole of awkward silence that poor Mr. Shelton struggled to fill by shoveling words—any words—into it: "Not that we're actually in church now. I mean, we're next door."

It was obvious he wanted something—adults usually do when they hang around trying to talk to kids—but I couldn't imagine what. Evan sensed it, too, but he was more direct. Or more merciful, maybe.

"Is there anything we can help you with, Mr. Shelton?" he asked pleasantly.

The man looked as relieved as if someone had told him, "You can stop hitting your head with that hammer now."

"Why, yes," he said, studying the ash on his shoes. "Yes, there sure is. Easter is coming right up, ya know, and I need somebody to, well, take charge of the pageant, and I think you two fellas would be perfect. Of course, nothing is weally perfect in this world, but you guys would come pwetty darned close."

And then *he* laughed, "Huh-huh-huh."

The Sunday school was responsible for two church services each year: the Christmas Eve service and the Easter sunrise service. That meant two unlucky kids always got the "privilege" of being in charge.

"Uh-oh," Evan said, "I think I hear my mother calling me."

"No, seriously," Mr. Shelton said. A big drop of

sweat fell onto his shoe, turning the ash to mud.

"I know it's a lot of wesponsibility, but I'll help you"—Evan shot me a quick, raised eyebrow look and I had to hide a smile—"but the service belongs to you youngsters and so we always like to put some of you in charge."

When neither of us replied, he swallowed hard and added a plaintive, "Pwease?"

He sounded pathetic and Evan must have been thinking the same thing because he squeezed the man's arm reassuringly and said, "Sure, we'll help, won't we, Andy?"

"Gee," I said sarcastically, "I don't see how I can say no, it sounds like such fun."

"Thanks, you guys," Mr. Shelton said. He was the only adult I knew who actually sounded humble.

He might have been humble but now that he had our promise, he was in a hurry, too: to get away before we changed our minds. He was still talking as he started to walk away.

"Maybe we can get together on Wednesday," he said over his shoulder, "for a wittle planning meeting. Yeah, that would be good. I'll see you then," he said. "Yeah, Wednesday would be good," he told the planter as he passed it. He was moving fast now. His shoes were going slap-slap-slap, like they were giving him a standing ovation. "After the evening service," he said, and almost ran into the kitchen to get out of our sight.

Evan grinned apologetically. "I'm sorry I got you into this," he said. "But I can't say no to Mr. Shelton. It'd be like snatching a bottle away from a starving baby."

"Yeah, well, just don't try to pick him up and burp him," I cautioned. "Or you'll get a double hernia."

Evan laughed. "You're a funny kid," he said, and ruffled my hair.

I blushed. "And you're a *nice* kid," I replied, reaching out an awkward hand to ruffle *his* hair.

Did I mention that his hair was the color of copper with gold streaks? Or that it was shoulder length? Or that sometimes he wore it in a ponytail, but that today it was loose, like a shower of sunlight?

I wasn't quite sure what his hair felt like as I touched it, like a fall of soft feathers, maybe, or an angel's wing—where did that thought come from, I wondered, and then remembered a poem Miss Flannegan used to read us in school: It was by James Whitcomb Riley, the Hoosier poet guy, and it was real corny but it had this one great line I'd never forgotten: "Like a flight of angel wings, winnowing the air."

Evan was looking at me quizzically and I realized that my hand was still resting on his halo of hair.

"Bless you, my son," I said, hoping some lame humor would rescue me from a situation that had just become unbearably awkward. And then I yanked my hand away as if it were resting on a hot stove.

"I'm sorry," I mumbled.

"Hey, it's okay," he said reassuringly. "People are always wanting to touch my hair."

"Yeah, sure," I mumble-mumbled, feeling as anxious as Mr. Shelton to slap-slap-slap away before I died of embarrassment. I was so busy looking for a trapdoor to speed up my exit that I didn't realize the Thornton Twins had fluttered up to us.

"Look at this beautiful hair, Velma," Thelma said, pointing at Evan's head. "Oh, I've just got to touch it."

And she did.

Evan grinned triumphantly and winked at me.

"See?" he said. And I laughed in relief and delight and, for some reason, I thought of my guardian angel for the first time since I had been a little boy. . . .

Three days later, I went to a wittle planning meeting with Evan, Mr. Shelton, and the old commander himself, Pastor Peterson.

"All right, men," the pastor barked at Evan and me as we sat at attention on the hard, straight-backed visitors' chairs in his spartan office. "This is not fun and games, now. This is the death and resurrection of our Lord."

"Yessir," we mumbled, trying to look solemn while Mr. Shelton shifted uncomfortably in the chair next to me. Parts of him were spilling precariously over the sides.

The pastor marched briskly back and forth behind his desk as if he were on a parade ground.

"Your mission," he continued, "is to convey, through this pageant, the solemnity and majesty of the occasion."

"And the joy, of course," Evan interrupted, as if he were just being helpful.

The pastor looked annoyed and about as joyful as a little kid who finds a switch and a lump of coal in his Christmas stocking.

"Of course," he said shortly. "But let's not forget the gravity of the responsibility you're undertaking. Coordinating all the elements of the pageant—recitations, music, tableau, costumes—will be like conducting a military campaign. Mr. Shelton will be your commanding officer, of course." (Field Marshall Fudd, I thought, and then felt ashamed of my casual cruelty). "Consider me the reserves. But don't call me up unless it's absolutely necessary. This is your pageant, not mine. Now, Logan." He turned his eagle eyes to me and I wondered if he expected me to salute. "You're good with words so you'll be in charge of the narrative portions of the pageant. Here are some sample programs we've used in the past."

He handed me a stack of folders.

"Follow their example. Stick with the tried and true. Easter is no time to be daring and original."

"Adams, you'll be in charge of the music."

Mr. Shelton coughed nervously.

"Oh," the pastor said. "With Marie's help, that is."

Marie was Mrs. Shelton, of course. She conducted the junior choir, which Evan called "Marie and the Monotones." Whenever the choir sang, Mrs. Shelton sang along, turning each of its songs into a solo for herself, since her powerful soprano easily drowned out the kids' spiritless, tentative whisperings.

"We'll make a joyful noise together," Evan said innocently.

The pastor stopped parading and looked peeved. "Listen, son," he told Evan between his teeth. "Let's not turn this pageant into a contest of wills, okay? Easter is a solemn occasion, not Bob Hope entertaining the troops. This is about God's sacrificing his only son on the cross to save us from our sins, okay?"

"Sure," Evan shrugged, "but—"

The pastor cut him off. "No buts," he said, looking at his watch. "You men have your marching orders. Go to it. Unless you have anything to add, Stanley?"

He gave Mr. Shelton a "you'd better not" look.

"No, no," Mr. Shelton said meekly. "You've said it all. C'mon, fewwows; we've got our work cut out for us."

"Yeah," Evan said, with mock enthusiasm, "it's our pageant, after all. Let's get busy."

He stood up and headed for the door. Mr. Shelton and I played follow the leader.

Neither of us dared to look back at the pastor.

"This is where we keep the pageant costumes," Mr. Shelton was saying as he slid a closet door open. We were standing in a small, dusty room at the far side of the altar.

Mr. Shelton pulled a costume out of the closet and blew dust off it. "Phew," he said, "it wooks like the moths have been into this one."

In fact, I thought, all the costumes looked pretty moth-eaten.

"Oh, wook at this one," Mr. Shelton said excitedly, "I wore this wise man costume when I was eight years old. Oops," he added as a sleeve fell off the costume and onto the floor.

"Time to give that one a decent burial," Evan said, poking around in the closet. "Actually, most of these look like they've seen better days."

"I'll talk to Patti about helping you," Mr. Shelton promised, wiping his damp forehead on the costume he was holding and leaving a streak of dirt on his face. "This'll be good experience for her. Her mother is teaching her to sew, ya know."

"She already told us," I said.

"Oh, okay," Mr. Shelton replied, turning to Evan. "Wisten," he said, "I'll talk to Marie about helping with the music, too."

"Tell her to keep it joyful," Evan replied, straight-faced.

"Well . . ." Mr. Shelton said dubiously, darting an uneasy look in the direction of the pastor's office.

"Just kidding," Evan reassured him, "just kidding."

Mr. Shelton looked relieved. "Pastor Pete takes all this pwetty seriously," he said. "But I know it's in good hands with you two. I'll leave you to it. You don't need an old fogey like me looking over your shoulders."

Like most things adults said, this required a translation. Fortunately I spoke excellent adult. What he really meant was, I'm passing the buck to you two because I don't want the responsibility. And besides, I'm tired and I want to go home and drink a beer, and the only reason I'm doing this in the first place is because my wife makes me so she can run the whole thing anyway.

"Okay," Evan said cheerfully.

"Goodnight," I added as Mr. Shelton shambled off.

He waved absently without turning around.

I was secretly glad that Mr. Shelton had left so I could have some time alone with Evan, even though it still made me feel nervous and awkward and afraid that I'd say something stupid or do something that would make him dislike me.

"That was really neat," I said shyly, "your standing up to the pastor about the joyful part of Easter. I wouldn't have had the guts."

"Sure you would have," Evan said with blessed assurance as he pulled an armload of costumes out of the closet.

Easy for him to say but I wasn't so sure.

"I mean," he continued, as he sorted through the costumes, "you've got to stand up for the things you believe in. And you've got to be true to yourself."

It would have sounded like lip service from anybody else, but I knew he meant it. In fact, he had created a stir at school the year before and had gotten suspended for a week when he organized an unauthorized peace march to protest the Vietnam War. He had been interviewed on local television and some of the older men in the congregation still referred to him as "that damn hippie" because of it. If Pastor Peterson could have suspended him from church, too, he would have, I bet. I wondered if I could ever be that brave . . . I doubted it.

"Boy, these costumes are a mess," Evan said. "Look at these."

He held up something flimsy, gauzy, and shapeless.

"What's that supposed to be?" I asked.

"A pair of wings, I think. They must have been part of an angel costume."

The limp, filmy fabric was covered with gold spangles, and the frayed edges were bordered with gold braid.

"Maybe they belonged to the guardian angel of the dime store," I said, wrinkling up my nose.

Evan laughed. "They're pretty tacky, aren't they?"

"Maybe they belonged to a fallen angel," I said.

Evan grinned and put the wings aside. "I'll have to make some new ones if you decide to have any respectable angels in your pageant," he said.

"Our pageant," I corrected.

"*Touché,*" Evan acknowledged. "I guess I am the one who got you into this. So," he continued, "how shall we proceed, Mr. Co-Chair?"

I winced. I hadn't expected he would look to me for direction. I thought it would be the other way around.

"Uh, well . . ." I started to dither. And he took mercy on me, as he had on Mr. Shelton. "Why don't you make me a list of characters you want to include? Then

I can start working on costumes for them and selecting some appropriate music."

He made it sound easy but I was beginning to realize the enormity of the undertaking.

"God," I groaned, "I've got to read through all those programs that the pastor gave me and try to pull together a pageant from them and then we've got to assign speaking parts and schedule rehearsals. And we've only got five weeks. And . . ."

I was starting to feel seriously overwhelmed.

"And the pastor will have you court-martialed if everything doesn't go just right," Evan teased.

"He probably will," I agreed gloomily.

"Hey," Evan protested, cheerful as always. "Not a chance. I'll protect you." He picked up the ruined wings and held them against his shoulders. "You see," he said conspiratorially, "though you may think I am only mild-mannered boy organist Evan Adams, in reality, I am . . ." he paused for dramatic effect ". . . GUARDIAN ANGEL MAN. Tah-dum."

And he flapped the wings as if he were going to fly around the room.

"My hero," I said, trying to sound sarcastic because, for some reason, I felt I had to hide how comforting I found the idea.

Or maybe it was some other feeling I was trying to hide? Whatever it was made me feel guilty and without even knowing why, I automatically hid my excitement from my family, too, pretending to be bored but resigned. Though my mother, at least, was as excited as I was.

"Just imagine," she bubbled. "Pageant co-chair with that nice Evan Adams. I'm so proud of you, Andy. Aren't you proud, Hal?"

"Yeah, sure," the old man grunted and opened another bottle of beer.

Easter pageant co-chair? my attitude asked. Well, it's a lousy job but someone's got to do it. A good old Christian martyr, that's me.

But secretly I couldn't wait for the following Wednesday evening to be with Evan again in the room off the altar. My excitement was tempered a bit by the fact that Patti-with-an-i was there, too. I wasn't enthusiastic about *that* but Mr. Shelton had insisted that she help us, though personally I figured the only help she could give us would be to talk until our ears fell off so she could practice sewing them back on.

But I was wrong.

To my surprise she really had learned how to sew. She was quick and efficient with a needle and she didn't need to be told what had to be done. Her square hands with their blunt fingers were . . . capable. And so busy that her mouth didn't have time to talk . . . much.

Evan's hands were busy, too. He had decided to make new wings for the angel costumes. He started by constructing frames out of light wood laths and then covering them with white cloth, sort of like kites. Now he was busy sewing feathers onto the cloth. If Patti's hands were capable, Evan's were beautiful, moving like a swift blessing over the wings. I was busy, too, trying to patch together a pageant out of bits and pieces of old programs. The hard part was finding enough Bible verses for all the kids whose parents would want them to have speaking parts. The rest of the kids, who were either too timid to speak in front of the congregation or just too dumb to memorize verses, would get non-speaking, costumed parts in the tableau.

The first rehearsal was held on a Saturday morning. It was one of those windy, unsettled days when flags spank the sky and the sun plays hide-and-seek with the scudding clouds. No one wanted to be stuck in a stuffy church on a spring day like that and the twenty or so kids who showed up were restless and uncooperative. Especially since there were no adults around to keep order. The Junior Choir always practiced separately, which meant Mrs. Shelton wasn't there to lock heels. And Mr. Shelton, who had at least been around at first, couldn't lock a door, let alone heels. But then even he had to leave to run errands for his wife. Meanwhile Evan headed for the room off the altar to continue working on costumes.

"Can I come, too?" Benjie Peterson piped eagerly. Because of his precarious health, he didn't get to participate a lot but his parents did let him come over from the parsonage next door to watch rehearsals. What he really wanted to watch, though, was Evan. I guess his father hadn't told him about the First Commandment, because Benjie clearly worshipped the older boy. Whenever Evan was present, Benjie followed him around like a skinny little disciple.

"Sure, I guess so," Evan said agreeably.

"Oh, boy," Benjie said, and ran after him.

After that things began to fall apart. I felt like I was trying to direct a play at a clown college. Kids were running up and down the aisles, hanging over the balcony, slugging each other, and generally ignoring my pleas to settle down.

"C'mon, guys," I hollered from my post behind the lectern. "We'll get out of here a lot quicker if you'll just cooperate."

"What's the matter, Boss?" Evan asked, poking his

head out of the costume room. "Patients taken over the asylum?"

"What do you think?" I asked gloomily, pointing at the hyperactive madhouse in front of us.

"Never fear," he grinned, "GUARDIAN ANGEL MAN is here. Tah-dum!" And he leaped dramatically out of the room. Benjie, of course, followed right behind, giggling like a little madman.

Putting two fingers in his mouth, Evan whistled piercingly. Benjie's hands flew to his ears, and there was a sudden shocked silence. I don't think any of the kids had ever heard a whistle in church before. I know I hadn't, and I guess they were as afraid as I was that God might suddenly appear to punish this blasphemy.

It didn't bother Evan, though. "Here's the deal," he told the suddenly silent crowd. "If you'll settle down and do what Andy tells you, the management—that's me—will provide some entertainment."

I don't know if it was the intriguing promise of entertainment or just the sudden presence of an older kid—and a fearless blasphemer, at that—but everybody eagerly crowded to the front of the church and took seats in the pews.

"How many of you can do this?" Evan asked his audience and did an elegant cartwheel and then another. "Or this?" he asked, doing a handstand and then walking on his hands around the altar.

The kids gasped appreciatively and applauded— Benjie loudest of all. I figured that if, to me, God looked like my father with a flaming sword, to Benjie he must have looked exactly like Evan did at that moment, miraculously walking on his hands.

"Let me try, let me try," the little boy demanded, as Evan leaped back to his feet. Benjie was already on his hands and knees, gamely trying to lift his legs up. But his arms were too weak to support his weight, and he kept falling over.

Evan grinned. "Better let me help you," he said. "Easy now." He grabbed Benjie's ankles and lifted his lower body up until it was fully extended—but upside down. Supporting Benjie's weight, Evan then walked him around the altar floor. From a distance it looked like Benjie was actually walking on his hands but in fact the tips of his fingers were half an inch off the floor. The kids in the pews laughed and applauded anyway.

Evan lowered the little boy's body to the floor and crouched down beside him.

"Here's something I'll bet you can really do," he said: "Stand on my shoulders."

Benjie looked uncertain, but Evan reassured him. "You can do it; you just have to believe you can. And besides, Andy'll help you."

And I did. I hoisted Benjie up so he was crouched with his feet on Evan's shoulders and his arms around Evan's forehead. Then, gathering his weight under him, Evan stood up and at the same time, I put my hands under Benjie's butt and pushed up upright so he was standing up. I held on to him so he wouldn't fall; Evan shouted, "*Alley-oop*;" Benjie shrieked with laughter, and the kids cheered.

That's when it happened. When everybody was excited and happy. That's when it always happens:

"STOP THAT CLOWNING AROUND," a voice from nowhere thundered. It sounded like a hungover God shouting at noisy neighbors and everybody jumped and looked fearfully around. It wasn't God, though, it was Pastor Peterson, but he was every bit as wrathful.

He stormed up the aisle from the back of the church where he had been silently watching us.

"Get down from that altar," he ordered. "That's God's sacred place. What you're doing there is blasphemy."

"Oh, it is not," Evan said. He sounded tired. He put Benjie down but the little boy clung to him as if he saw a hurricane coming and Evan was a sturdy tree he could hold on to.

"WHAT!" the pastor demanded, his eyes bulging like bad eggs.

"The kids were tired," Evan explained. "We were just giving them a break."

"By desecrating God's altar?" the pastor demanded, beginning to sputter like a ticking bomb ready to explode.

"I doubt God thinks a few harmless acrobatics are a desecration," Evan replied calmly.

"I'll tell you what God thinks!" the pastor said. "He thinks you're a blasphemer and a wiseass. And I don't even like to think what else—with your fancy long hair and your sissy peace marches."

Sometimes I wondered if there really was a God. But I never, ever doubted that there was a devil, and I prayed that right about now he was grinning and painting a big "Welcome Home" sign down in hell for the pastor.

I don't know what Evan was thinking. I only know he didn't say anything. He just stared at the pastor, who glowered back. The tension was terrible, like a big hand choking us.

Finally, mercifully, one of the little kids in the front pew started to cry and the pastor's concentration was broken. He looked away from Evan, out at the crying kid, and then at Benjie.

"I'm ashamed of you," he snapped. "My own son taking part in this blasphemy."

Benjie started to shake. If Evan was a tree, he was a leaf and the storm was blowing hard now.

"Go home this instant," the pastor ordered. "We'll talk about your punishment later."

Benjie let go of Evan, turned, and ran obediently for the side door. When it slammed shut behind him, the pastor turned to the kids cowering in the pews.

"I don't want any more of this nonsense," he said, his voice sounding as if it were pounding nails. "Understood?"

There were only a few timid "yessirs" but enough, apparently, to satisfy him, since he turned away from them and back to Evan—and to me.

"It's too late to pick new chairmen for the pageant," he said sourly, "or—believe me—you two clowns would be out of here."

"Don't blame Andy," Evan said. "This was my idea."

The pastor was unforgiving. "That's not good enough. He should have stopped you. You're co-chairs. You're both responsible. I promise you if there's a recurrence of this kind of behavior, there will be no pageant and I'll not hesitate to explain to the congregation exactly why. Is that understood?"

Evan continued to stare silently at him. But I wasn't that brave. "Yessir," I said, my voice sounding like a bowl of Jell-o in an earthquake.

"Good," the pastor said. His jaw muscles bulged as if they were lifting weights. "I'll be watching both of you," he grunted, and marched away to his office.

"Jesus," I whispered when he was gone. I felt like I had just run ten miles.

"Jesus has nothing to do with it," Evan said. He squeezed the back of my neck affectionately.

"Okay, everybody," he told the kids. "Entertainment's over. Back to work." He clapped his hands briskly and the rehearsal resumed. The sun, which had been streaming through the stained glass windows, went behind a cloud or maybe it was the pastor's long shadow that turned all of us into creatures who dwell in darkness for the rest of the morning.

The rehearsal went off without a hitch, though. And without one second of joy.

• • •

It was a good thing school was easy for me. If I'd had to spend a lot of time studying, I'd have been a dead duck because the pageant was devouring my days. I had to take care of a lot of the stuff by myself. Evan was a senior, after all, and too busy to help much. When he wasn't working, he was studying or training for the gymnastics team. Now that I was getting to know him, I ran with him sometimes, early in the morning, but even though he had invited me, I always felt like a pesty little brother tagging along. So I usually made some lame excuse not to join him and ran by myself someplace else. And wished I was with him the whole time. I started thinking about him during class, wondering what he was doing while I was diagramming dreary sentences. Fantasizing that my parents had had another kid and it had been Evan and he was MY big brother not Eddie's. And, for a second, I'd feel like Benjie, standing on Evan's shoulders, close enough to heaven to touch it. I even started to dream about him. In my dream I was always running through darkness, away from some enormously dark something—or someone—with flames for eyes and lots of grabbing hands with fingernail claws that reached out to rip me apart. Faster and faster, I'd run, heart pounding my chest to pieces, but I knew I could never run fast enough to escape it, whatever it was. But at the last second, tah-dah, my guardian angel flew down out of the sky on wings of sunshine, reached out strong arms and lifted me up from the clutching hands and the fiery eyes, and carried me up into another world of sky and sun, a warmly bright world where I was safe and secure in the sheltering arms of my guardian angel, whose face I could look at, at last, and discover it was Evan. And I wasn't a bit surprised. Just happy. Because I knew that after all my running, I had finally reached my destination.

Until I woke up. And then I was right back where I had started. And the old man was throwing up on the rug outside my room. In the darkness . . .

It was storming when I got up the following Saturday morning.

"Oh, man," I groaned to Mother, "how am I going to get to church? I promised Evan I'd meet him there at eleven o'clock."

"Well, I'd take you," Mother offered, finishing her coffee at the kitchen table, "but I have to go shopping with Grandma Logan."

She looked like she'd rather take poison.

"She's picking me up in a few minutes," Mother continued. "Maybe your father can drive you."

Now it was my turn to look like *I'd* rather take poison.

"Well, you can't walk there in this weather," she said. "It's time he got up, anyway. It's already nine thirty."

"Oh, God, he'll kill me," I moaned.

"Oh, don't be silly," Mother said; "he won't do any such thing. I'll go wake him up now."

She got up from the table and I jumped up, too, and followed her into the living room trying to stop her as she headed down the hall and vanished into the bedroom. I stood in the empty living room, my shoulders slumped in defeat, hearing her raise the window shade and start calling my father's name.

I shuddered involuntarily. Trying to wake my father up in the morning was about as easy—and dangerous—as trying to rouse a bear out of hibernation in midwinter.

"Hal, Hal," I heard my mother say.

I didn't hang around to hear his reaction. I hurried back into the kitchen and sat down at the table and looked out the window at the raindrops pelting down like little boxing gloves pounding the earth.

There was a flash of lightning, a clap of thunder, and an equally thunderous, "AW, SHIT!" from my father.

Thanks, Mother, I thought. Thanks a lot. He's really gonna be in a great mood to take me to church now.

Then there was an urgent honking outside. It sounded like a dozen demented geese.

HONKHONKHONKHONK.

More thunder.

Another loud "Aw, shit," from the bedroom.

HONKHONKHONKHONK. Grandma was her usual patient self.

"I'm coming, I'm coming," I heard my mother say breathlessly. And then I heard her running down the hallway.

"Andy," she called from the living room, "I'm leaving now. Your father will take you to church."

I heard the front door open. And close. And then my father, chased out of his cave of sleep, lumbered into the kitchen. He glowered at me with bloodshot, hungover eyes.

"I gotta go to church," he said in a nasty, mocking voice.

I knew better than to say anything. Sometimes even an "I'm sorry" would set him off. And then there would be a storm inside to match the one raging outside. Muttering to himself my father poured a cup of coffee and sat down heavily at the table across from me. He was wearing nothing but his boxer shorts. His naked shoulders and chest were as huge and hairy as a bear's. And his beer gut spilled over the top of his shorts. His face, his neck, and his arms were sunburned from working outside in a T-shirt, but the rest of his body was as white as something you'd find under a rock.

I stared fixedly out the window so I wouldn't have to look at him and listened, instead, to him slurping his coffee. I couldn't bear being alone in the same room with him, but I was afraid to get up and leave without an acceptable excuse. Which I didn't have. So I just sat there in miserable silence, my stomach feeling like a clenched fist.

Finally finishing his coffee, the old man hoisted himself up, rinsed his cup out, and without saying anything more to me, walked heavily out of the room.

I looked at the clock. It was ten now. We'd have to leave in forty-five minutes if I was to get to church on time. I exhaled in relief, hearing the shower start and realized I'd been holding my breath. I went into my bedroom and got a cap and my raincoat from the closet. I put them on the chair by the front door, so

I'd be ready when the old man finally deigned to drive me to church.

I heard the bathroom door open. "What time do you have to be there?" he called.

"At eleven," I said.

"Yeah, okay," he muttered.

I heard him leave the bathroom then and lurch down the hall to his bedroom.

I thought about waiting for him in the chair by the door but I knew that would only make it look like I was rushing him, so instead, I went back into the kitchen and sat down by the window. It was raining harder than ever.

At precisely ten after ten the old man reappeared in the doorway. He was dressed to go outside, and I started to get up. We'd be early, I thought, but at least I'd be there.

"Where do you think you're going?" he demanded.

"Aren't we going to church?" I asked in confusion.

"Hell, no," he scowled, looking at me like I was crazy. "It's only ten o'clock."

"Twelve after ten," I corrected him silently.

"I gotta go someplace else first," he said. "I'll be back by ten forty-five to get you."

I collapsed into the chair. I'd never get to church on time now, I thought gloomily. I knew where "someplace else" was. It was the Jolly Tap, his favorite bar, and once the old man got to *that* someplace, he might not get back until ten forty-five at night.

After he left the house, I got a book and tried to read but I kept looking up at the clock and losing my place. And then I'd have to start the same page all over again. After about the fifteenth time, I shut the book and simply sat.

And waited.

And waited.

I pushed the chair back desperately and got up and walked to the living room window and stood, looking out at the wall of rain and trying to will my father to come home and drive me to church. But by the time eleven o'clock rolled around, my will was worn out and I was desperate. And so I did something equally desperate: I decided to walk to church after all. My father had obviously forgotten all about me, I told myself, as I put on my hat and coat. And even if he did come home to find me gone, I rationalized, he'd be relieved to find that he didn't have to drive me to church after all and could go back to the bar.

I stepped out into the rain and, half-running and half-walking, set off for church.

• • •

By the time I had gone half a block, I was soaked to the skin. My mother had taken our only umbrella, so the rain poured down the back of my neck. I splashed through a puddle with every other step. The wind blew the rain around me like a clingingly wet shower curtain. But I didn't care, I was on my way to see Evan.

So focused was I on this warm, sunshiny thought that I didn't see the Dentmobile pull up to the curb beside me. And I wasn't aware of my father's getting out until I heard him shout, "HEY!"

I turned around and saw him headed for me. I could tell by the way he walked that he was already half-drunk. He didn't lurch or stagger when he was drunk. He stood ramrod straight like one of Pastor Peterson's marines. And he marched instead of walked.

Left, right, left, right, he came toward me.

"What the hell do you think you're doing," he shouted at me.

Nothing I could say would save me now.

He loomed over me.

"Answer me," he shouted. He grabbed me by the shoulder and shook me.

"I'm sorry," I pleaded, hearing the panic in my voice. "I thought you'd forgotten me."

"WHAT?" he roared.

"I thought you'd forgotten me."

"Goddam you," he shouted. "I leave what I'm doing, drive all the way home, and find that you didn't even have the decency to wait for me. Who the hell do you think you are?"

Your beloved son in whom you're well pleased? I thought frantically before he slapped me. Hard. I saw stars and my knees buckled.

"Shit," he fumed, yanking me to my feet. "See what you made me do?"

The rain beating against my cheek stung. I put my hand against it and saw blood when I took it away.

"Here," the old man said, handing me his handkerchief. "Hold it against that cut."

Then: "Get in the car," he ordered roughly.

I realized his high school football ring had cut my cheek when he'd hit me. Even with the handkerchief against it, it still stung. The old man got in the car. He seemed soberer now. Maybe hitting me had scared him. Or maybe it was just standing outside in the cold rain that had done it.

"Be more considerate of other people next time," he said. And the car became a classroom in which didactic Dad became a teacher instructing me in the niceties of interpersonal relationships. "Don't always be thinking only of yourself," he lectured.

"Yessir," I mumbled.

We drove the rest of the way to church in awkward silence, pulling up in front of the Parish Hall where he thrust some money into my hand. "Call a cab when you're ready to come home," he said. "I have to go someplace."

"Yessir," I mumbled. I got out and watched the tail-lights of the car as he drove away.

Through the still pouring rain.

"Hey," Evan said, smiling a warming welcome as I walked into the church library at last. "There you are. I was getting worried about you."

Then he got a good look at me.

"God, what happened to you?" he demanded, pulling my hand and the handkerchief it held away from my cheek.

"I've told you and told you," he said with mock seriousness, "no more dueling. I guess I'm just going to have to lock up those sabers."

"I had to rescue the neighbor's cat from the rain," I said. "And it scratched me."

Being my father's son had made me an expert impromptu liar. But it hadn't taught me how not to feel guilty as hell whenever I mangled the truth.

Evan took the handkerchief out of my hand and dabbed gently at my cheek. "It's not as bad as I thought," he said. "But, God, you're all wet, too!" he exclaimed, examining me more closely. "Did you walk here?"

"Yes," I said. "No. Well, halfway anyway."

Evan started rubbing my hair dry with the handkerchief and suddenly I felt overwhelmed. By his kindness, maybe, or by the old man's unthinking, unexamined cruelty. Or maybe it was both.

"Shit," I said, collapsing into a chair. "I wish he was dead."

"Who, the cat?" Evan asked.

"No. My fucking father."

There was an awkward silence. I could feel Evan's eyes looking down at the top of my head.

Then, softly, he asked, "Did you know that my father killed himself?"

"Oh, God, I'm sorry," I said rushingly. "I didn't even know you'd had a father."

It was a dumb apology, but at least it made Evan laugh and relieved the sudden awkward tension between us.

"Right," he grinned. "And three wise men showed up at my crib bearing gifts when I was born."

"I'm sorry," I blushed. "That was a stupid thing for me to say."

"No it wasn't," Evan reassured me. "You never knew him. He was already dead when we moved here."

"How old were you when he . . ." my voice trailed off.

"When he committed the unpardonable sin?" Evan asked. "About eight. Eddie was five, I guess."

"Why did he do it"? I asked.

"Who knows?" Evan shrugged. "For a long time I guess I thought it was my fault. I felt pretty lousy about it."

"Why would you think it was YOUR fault?" I demanded.

He didn't answer for a minute, and I was afraid I shouldn't have asked.

But then he said, "I've never told anybody this. I mean, it's really hard to talk about."

"You don't have to tell me," I blurted.

"No, I want to. See, here's the thing: My dad used to, well . . ." He had to look away to finish, ". . . play with me. You know what I mean?"

I didn't, exactly. But I sure knew it wasn't baseball he was talking about.

"Sexually," he concluded, relentless in his need to tell me.

I struggled to find something to say. And here's what I came up with: "I guess maybe fathers do bad stuff to kids sometimes. I mean, my old man hits me, y'know? He slapped me just this morning. That's where this stupid scratch came from. It wasn't the neighbor's cat. It was his ring hitting me."

I hoped my confession would help, but Evan wasn't finished yet. He looked at me searchingly. "Did you want him to?"

"Huh?" I said stupidly.

"Did you want him to slap you?"

"Of course not," I said, still not understanding.

"Well, I did. Want my dad to. To . . . play with me."

The words came out all twisted and there was this awful silence between us.

For a second all I could think of was my old man doing something like that to me, and I felt like I was going to throw up.

"I know you think that's sick," Evan said plead-ingly. "But I couldn't help it. I don't know why I wanted him to. I can't understand it even now. I've never understood it. Except that maybe it was the only way I could be sure he loved me. Or needed me."

Sitting next to me, telling me this, Evan looked like something beautiful that someone had callously broken into a thousand ugly pieces. And I wanted desperately to put them back together again. To restore the beauty. But I had no glue, and I had no skillful fingers; all I had were clumsy words and the only ones of those I could think to say were these: "My Uncle Charles thought that the heart has reasons the mind can't know. I never knew for sure what that meant but maybe it was just that we all need to be loved. So sometimes we do things we can't understand to get it. But that doesn't mean we're bad people or that it's our fault when other people do bad things *to us* in the name of love. I remember my mother used to tell me that my old man hit me because he loved me and wanted me to do the right thing."

Who was I trying to convince, I wondered then, Evan or me? Because in my own most secret heart, I realized that I had always felt it was my fault that my old man did the things he did. That if I could only be a better person, if I could only do the right thing, he wouldn't drink anymore or rage or hit me. And every time he did, it was just more evidence that Andy was being a bad boy. And who would love a bad boy?

But for just this one moment what I said seemed to help Evan anyway, because he grabbed me and hugged me impulsively, holding me tight. "Thanks," he whispered, and I felt the word imprinted on my cheek as his hair fell forward on either side of my face and I felt like I was in a secret room somewhere with him where no one else could go, and I felt so safe there with him. I wanted to stay in that room forever, with his arms around me, but I couldn't, of course. He had to let me go. And he did.

But not before I realized that now MY heart had not only found its own reasons but maybe, just maybe, a friend, at last.

Like Angel Wings, Part ii

Like Angel Wings, Part ii

No matter how much I complained, there were things I liked about church: the building itself, for one, because it was so old that when I sat inside, I felt connected—to the past and to all the people who had sat there before me. For another, the simple beauty of the sanctuary, its rows of hand-carved wooden pews worn smooth by generations of bodies and its vaulted ceiling reaching for the sky. I liked the ornate beauty of the stained-glass windows and I liked the massive bells and the sound of their being rung in the steeple, calling the faithful to worship. And I liked the rich, rumbling sound of the organ that began at the last bell's peal; I liked the formal liturgy that followed. But most of all, I suppose, I liked the reassuring, comforting familiarity of it all. I knew the liturgy by heart—not because I had made a point of memorizing it but because it never varied; it was so . . . *predictable*. Everything else in my life changed but church was as unchanging as the three-foot-thick stone walls that supported its slate roof.

Until the night Evan stood up in the middle of the service, that is, and forced everything to change—forever.

It was the fourth Wednesday in Lent. During the season preceding Easter my church had an evening service not only on Ash Wednesday but on every Wednesday that followed right up through Holy Week. Each year Pastor Peterson chose a different theme to unify his sermons throughout the entire season. One year it was Jesus' words on the cross. Another year it was the passion history presented from the viewpoint of various biblical participants—Pontius Pilate, Judas, Simon Peter, and the rest.

This year he was preaching about the seven deadly sins. As he pompously explained when he introduced the theme: "The seven deadly sins seem singularly appropriate, thematically speaking, to the season in which we remember that Jesus Christ gave up His life on the cross to provide the only sacrifice of a magnitude sufficient to atone for the unimaginable enormity of our sins."

I wanted to ask why, if we're so sinful, God didn't just squash us like bugs and get it over with, but I didn't dare and the pastor went right on raving about the very paschal lamb and the holy, innocent, bitter sufferings and death of our beloved Lord, but we in the congregation had already gotten the message. As usual, Pastor Pete had chosen some real pulpit-pounding stuff. Talk about the familiar, I thought.

He started off slowly with the tamer sins—warming up with sloth, pride, and gluttony. But now that Lent was more than half over, he was starting down the home stretch with the juicy stuff, the sins that brought high ratings in terms of attendance. Tonight it was lust.

The text for his sermon was Revelations 2:14. I remember because I was an altar boy that evening. Which meant I had to wear a white robe, light the candles during the opening hymn, snuff them out during the closing hymn, and in between sit in the big, uncomfortable wooden chair on the right side of the altar, where everybody in the congregation could see me. In other words I had to stay awake and pay attention even though my eyes weren't cooperating; they kept straying to Evan, who was sitting down in front in the first pew. Eddie was on one side of him and Benjie and Mrs. P. were on the other. My mother was sitting next to Mrs. P. at the end of the row on the center aisle. Best seat in the house. Next to mine, that is.

As the pastor stood in the pulpit reading his sermon text, I observed that Mother, Mrs. P., and Evan were dutifully watching him. Benjie, of course, was watching Evan (as was I), and Eddie was watching the inside of his eyelids.

The pastor finished reading his text ". . . by committing sexual immorality" and I sighed. I knew from past experience it was going to be a long sermon, filled with words that began with the letter L—words like lust, lasciviousness, licentiousness, and lubricity. I'd heard them all before. I tore my eyes away from Evan and dutifully fixed them on Pastor Peterson, who closed his Bible and actually rubbed his hands together in anticipation.

"Lust," he said. "Lasciviousness, licentiousness, lubricity. The sins of the sullied flesh."

He made them sound like headlines on the front page of the *National Enquirer,* and the congregation, large for a midweek service, leaned forward in anticipation of a good show. And the pastor gave it to them— a whole laundry list of vividly described sexual depravity: adultery; long-haired, hippie free love (he looked sourly at Evan); rock musicians and harlots (I wasn't sure if he thought they were the same or if maybe harlots was the name of a new band); blue movies (he named quite a few titles and I wondered how he knew about them); and finally, as if he had been saving the best for the last: "the love" (he sneered at the word) "that dares not speak its name. But you know what it is," he thundered. He picked up his Bible and opened it to a place he had marked: "Romans," he said, "chapter 1, verse 27: And likewise also the men," he read, "leaving the natural use of the woman, burned in their lust one toward another; men with men working that which is unseemly, and receiving in themselves that recompense of their error which was meet."

"Recompense," he said, savoring the word as if it tasted sweet as a spoonful of sugar.

"The marines know about recompense. Do you know what they do to—I hesitate to call them men—those who practice this most perverted of sexual sins? They court-martial them and kick them out of the corps with a dishonorable discharge. They cast them out. God knew even better what to do with them: He didn't simply cast them out; He destroyed them and their city of Sodom with fire and brimstone. He gave them a foretaste of the eternal hell fire that will be theirs unless they repent. For, as Saint Paul also says, 'In their lust for one another, they burn.' Well, I tell you, dear friends in Christ, all these practitioners of perversion, these—I'll say the word even though there are children present—these sodomites, these homosexuals, will burn not in lust but in the flames of eternal hell. For God *hates* homosexuals and their unspeakably evil perversions."

He had been talking faster and faster and louder and louder and now, suddenly, he paused for dramatic effect and into that sudden silence slipped the calm

sound of another voice saying, simply, "That's not true."
And Evan stood up and faced the pastor.

It was a surreal moment. For in the formality of our order of service where we did everything by the book, just like the Marines, the congregation's voices were not heard except in those responses printed in the hymnal. And it was inconceivable that one of those should come in the middle of a sermon. No one had ever, ever uttered a word—not even an impassioned "hallelujah" the way they did in the Baptist church across the street—during the pastor's sermon. Until now. People didn't know what to make of it. Some of them, I believe, thought it was a setup. Some clever routine the pastor had planned and enlisted that nice young Evan Andrews to help with. That might have explained the few expectant grins I saw here and there among the congregation. But they faded quickly enough when the pastor, plainly furious, swung around to Evan and demanded, "How dare you interrupt me? How dare you interrupt God? He is talking through me."

"I don't think so," Evan said.

The pastor's face turned as purple as an eggplant, and for a second I thought he was going to explode. He managed a strangled "WHAT" and then placed his hands on the rim of the pulpit and leaned forward, gasping for breath.

People began edging fearfully away from Evan as if they were chickens and he was a fox in the henhouse.

"I don't think God is talking through you," Evan continued calmly—"at least not when you say He hates homosexuals. I don't believe for a minute that He does. I think you do, though. I think that's why you're telling so many lies about them."

The pastor had partially recovered while Evan was

saying this. And he was thinking fast. It was almost like his brain was clockwork sitting on top of his head and you could see all the cogs and wheels spinning around at breakneck speed. Spinspinspin. He stood up straight, then, in his elevated pulpit and stared down at Evan like he was God in heaven looking down on a lost soul in hell.

"How can you say I'm telling lies?" he asked. "How can a boy your age know anything about such a terrible perversion?"

It was supposed to sound casually dismissive, what he said, but it was meant as a challenge. I knew it. Everybody knew it. Evan most of all.

There was a sudden silence as terrible as if someone had just pitched forward dead in front of us all.

And then Evan said it. As if there were no alternative. As if he had been predestined since the dawn of time to say it.

"I know it," he said, "because *I'm* a homosexual."

That's what he said, all right. And I sat in that big chair on the altar and looked at the reactions. At Eddie, who stared at his brother with his mouth so far open, I thought his brains would fall out. At my mother, who gasped and clutched Mrs. P.'s arm. At Benjie and the frightened, puzzled look on his face and at his mother, who reached out a comforting arm and pulled him to her. At the old Thornton twins, who obviously hadn't heard a word and were still smiling benignly at Evan. At Mr. Shelton, who mopped his brow and at Mrs. Shelton, who shot a thin-lipped look at Evan as if his head were on the chopping block now, all right. And at poor Patti-with-an-i who slumped down in her seat as if her heart were broken. And I realized suddenly that she was in love with Evan.

And, finally, at the pastor: He was looking at Evan with a big mask of mournfulness on his face. But you could see his eyes through the mask and in them there was a glint of triumph. I saw it. And I know Evan did, too.

"You poor, confused boy," the pastor said unctuously. "You don't know what you're saying."

"Yes, I do," Evan said stubbornly.

"Then for God's sake," the pastor said, with dramatic urgency. "Ask Him to forgive you now before it's too late. With His help, you can change your ways. Repent. Here and now."

"I don't have anything to repent," Evan said, more stubbornly still. "I haven't done anything sinful. And there is nothing wrong with who I am."

"What more can I say, then?" the pastor asked the congregation, throwing his hands up in mock defeat. "The Holy Ghost can extend an invitation, but anyone can choose not to RSVP. That's the glory and the burden of free will. If this poor, misguided boy won't ask for help, let *us* ask God's merciful help on his behalf."

He motioned with his hands, and everyone stood up. "Let us bow together in prayer," he said.

And heads bowed obediently. Eyes closed. But before mine did, I saw Evan shake *his* head and then stride down the side aisle. His eyes were wide open and his head was held high as he walked out the front door of the church and into the night that waited for him.

• • •

Mother and I drove home in awkward silence after the service. I figured she was too embarrassed to say anything and I wouldn't have known what to reply if she had. So as soon as we got home, I excused myself and went to bed. I turned the light out and lay there, studying my memory picture of Evan standing up in church, and I didn't know what to think.

Or maybe I did but didn't WANT to think it.

When I heard Evan say, I'm a homosexual, it was like a final piece had fallen into place in a really complicated picture puzzle. You figured you already knew what the puzzle depicted but you couldn't be absolutely sure until that last piece had been tried and found to fit. And then it was crystal clear what you were looking at. It was Evan and he was gay. But that wasn't what I was trying to avoid thinking about. The thought that stubbornly kept demanding my consideration was this: that I wasn't looking at a picture puzzle but at a mirror, instead. And when I looked at Evan in it, I was looking at myself. And seeing that I was gay, too. But that thought was too enormous and terrifying to comprehend. So I thought about other things. About the jokes I had heard guys tell at school; about those same guys putting other guys down by calling them faggots and lisping and making their wrists limp; about Billy asking Eddie who his date was that time I had had to go to the movies with him; and, of course, about Pastor Peterson's sermon and about being damned to eternal hell fire.

And then I thought about Evan and how good he was and kind and smart and brave and I realized that all the other stuff was bullshit. Or if it wasn't, if it was true, then Evan wasn't gay. He couldn't be. After all he wasn't anything like the awful things people said about gay men. None of it made any sense. And I knew that I could spend the rest of my life trying to figure it out. Wrestling with all these thoughts finally wore me out and I drifted off to sleep. Only to be awakened by the sound of my bedroom door being opened and the overhead light being turned on.

"Andy," my mother called softly, "are you awake?"

I grunted and shielded my eyes against the light with the back of my hand.

"Your father and I need to talk to you," she said, and I realized the old man was standing behind her. She sat down on the bed; the old man remained standing, looming over me.

"It's about Evan," she said, trying to look reassuring but only succeeding in looking as nervous as hell.

"What?" I asked. Now *I* was nervous as hell.

"Well," she said, "we know you've been spending quite a lot of time with him working on the Easter pageant, and we, well, we just . . ." her voice trailed off and she looked to the old man for help.

He was real helpful, all right.

"Has he tried any funny stuff with you?" he demanded roughly. "Because if he has, I'll kill the faggot son of a bitch."

"We were just concerned that if he had," my mother finally found her voice to say, "you might be afraid to tell us. Or you might think you needed to protect him."

"He doesn't need to be protected," the old man rasped, "he needs to be locked up, the sick bastard."

It was like he and my mother were having two different conversations. But somehow they got to the same place.

"We just think it would be good if you didn't see him anymore," Mother said.

"If he comes sniffing around, you tell me," the old man said. "I'll rip his nuts off. That's what should be done to all those fruits. That'd fix 'em."

"But what about the pageant," I mumbled, "church, and—"

"I don't think he'll be coming back to church," Mother said. She patted my hand, as if the thought should be reassuring. "And I'll talk to Mr. Shelton about the pageant. Don't worry about that. Just try to forget all of this . . . unpleasantness."

"Don't tell him that," my father growled. "He needs to be on the lookout. Those fruits try to recruit kids."

I had a sudden irreverent picture of Pastor Peterson looking like Uncle Sam in a Marine uniform, pointing his finger at the world and saying, the fruits want you. But I knew better than to say anything like that around the old man. Sarcasm with him only got me a belt in the head.

"Hear me?" the old man demanded.

"Yessir," I mumbled.

"Just . . . be careful," my mother said. She smiled wanly at me. "And try to get a good night's sleep."

She leaned forward and kissed me on the forehead. Then she got up and, pushing the old man ahead of her ("Yeah, be careful," he was saying), left the room, turning out the light as she closed the door.

Yeah, I thought. Be careful.

Or they might find out about you.

Somehow I finally went back to sleep. And discovered that your subconscious mind doesn't know anything about being careful. Because that night it gave me my first wet dream in months.

And it was about Evan.

●   ●   ●

Of course, everybody was talking about "it" the next day at school. You could stand in the hall and see the news spread like a forest fire. Someone would rush up to someone else and whisperwhisperwhisper in their ear and then you'd see a mouth form the word "no." Whisperwhisperwhisper and both people would rush off then to whisperwhisperwhisper in someone else's ear.

Steady Evan moved through it all, ignoring it and somehow finding the strength or the courage or the grace to simply be himself. Smiling, friendly. As if nothing had happened.

But, of course, something HAD happened. And no one—except Evan—knew how to react. Oh, there was the usual stuff: by eight o'clock in the morning someone had written the word "faggot" all over Evan's locker. Some kids laughed when he walked by. Some guys made kissing noises or worse: Some pointed at their crotches and said stupid stuff like, "Hey, Evan, come and get it." Some of the girls acted like they'd been personally insulted—I guess they were the ones who had had crushes on him, and now they felt rejected. But Evan ignored it all. And maybe—just maybe—it might have blown over. If only people hadn't started teasing Eddie, asking him if "it" ran in the family; or if he and Evan "did it" together. And then on Friday Billy Curtis waited until there was a big crowd of kids around, and when Evan walked past, he grabbed Eddie and kissed him on the cheek and then pretended to be all confused and flustered, putting his hand to his mouth and saying, "Ooops, oh, I do so hope I didn't make Evan jealous."

"Fuck you!" Eddie shouted. "And fuck you, too!" he screamed at Evan. "You fuckin' faggot, you've ruined my fuckin' life."

And to everybody's embarrassment he started to cry, making horrible, angry, sobbing sounds.

Evan came over and tried to put his arm around Eddie. But the younger brother shook his arm off.

"Leave me alone," he sobbed, and then ran away, brokenly, down the hall.

The crowd broke up in embarrassed confusion after that. But Evan stood, unmoving and alone, looking at the empty hall where Eddie had run.

•   •   •

On Saturday we had another rehearsal for the pageant. With Easter only eight days away, a scattering of adults had started to show up. Mrs. Shelton was finally there, shouting instructions at the junior choir. Mrs. P. was there, too, listening to kids rehearse their speaking parts. My mother was in the room off the altar helping Patti with costumes. The unfinished wings Evan had been building were leaning against the wall looking lonely.

They weren't alone: I went looking for Evan. No luck. Instead, I found Mr. Shelton downstairs in the parish hall repainting the tomb of Jesus—a cloth flat with a plywood backing. I was surprised to see Eddie helping him. Eddie looked like *he* belonged in the tomb. He was as pale as bleach. His eyes were as red as his hair and there were dark, half-moon circles under them. I knew better than to ask *him* where Evan was, so I continued my solo search. I looked in the library and the Sunday school classrooms but they were all empty. I finally went back to the church and climbed up the stairs to the organ loft. There was someone there but it wasn't Evan. It was a woman I didn't recognize until she turned around and I realized it was Mrs. Adams.

No wonder I hadn't recognized her. She no longer looked like the Queen of the Gypsies. Now she looked like the queen of the widows in mourning. She was wearing a plain black sweatshirt and loose-fitting black slacks. Her crazy cloud of red hair was pulled severely back from her face and crowded into a bun at the back of her neck. She wasn't wearing any makeup and, for the first time ever, no jewelry! She looked like someone had mugged her and stolen her personality. She even talked in a whisper. As if she was in church. Of course she was but that had never turned her volume down before.

"Oh, hello, Andrew," she whispered.

"Hi, Mrs. Adams," I said uneasily. "Is—uh, Evan here?"

At first I thought she wasn't going to answer me. She just looked at me as if she didn't know who I was talking about. And then she said, "No."

Just, "no." No words of explanation about the whereabouts of my missing co-chair or whether he would show up later. Or whether he had died and that's why she was wearing black. Just, "no."

"Oh," I said.

Just, "oh."

And I turned around and went back downstairs. Just in time to hear Mrs. Shelton holler up at Mrs. Adams, "We're ready to start."

And then I heard the organ begin to play, and as I stepped into the sanctuary, the sound of Mrs. Shelton stridently singing "I Am Jesus' Little Lamb" nearly blew me over.

Everybody seemed to be busy doing something that didn't involve me—rehearsing, sewing, singing, mumbling, painting. I wondered what Evan was doing and, deciding to find out, I slipped out the front door of the church and walked around to the side street. After peering through the parish hall's glass door and confirming that Eddie was still downstairs, I ran across the

street on tiptoes and up the walk to the Adams' run-
down little house. I knocked on the door. At first I
thought no one was home because it was so quiet
inside. But I knocked again, and this time I heard footsteps. Then the door opened. And Evan looked out.

"Hi," I said as brightly as Captain Kangaroo.
"Aren't you coming to rehearsal?"

"No," he said as flatly and dully as his mother had.
And I wondered for a second if the whole family had
been turned into zombies. But no. Not Evan.

"I'm sorry," he said then. He looked over my
shoulder and when he saw no one was there, he
grabbed my arm and pulled me inside.

"I'm sorry," he said again. "I can't help you anymore."

He explained why: "Pastor Peterson told Mother
she'd lose her job as organist if I set foot in the church
again without first making a public recantation. I told
her she'd better start checking the temperature in hell.
When it was a cold day there, I'd do it. Anyway," he
added, "you shouldn't be seen with me. People will
think"—he paused—and then said, "stuff."

"I don't care," I said.

"Well, you should. People can hurt you."

I looked at him. He looked sad. And I wanted so
badly to tell him something. If I could only turn the hug
he had given me the Saturday before into words. And
give them back to him like a gift. But I couldn't. Or
maybe I was just afraid to try. So the only word I gave
him was, "okay."

And I went back to church and to the rehearsal.

●　　●　　●

It was the following Tuesday afternoon, and there I
was, sitting in the bleachers at the gym. I was waiting for

a gymnastics meet to start, the first one to be scheduled since what my mother now referred to in a hushed voice as "the incident at church" and I was nervous as hell.

We didn't have a big high school and we certainly didn't have a big gymnastics team. In fact, we probably wouldn't have had one at all if Evan hadn't gotten interested in the sport when he was a freshman. His popularity guaranteed that enough other guys would follow his lead to form a team, which had turned out to be at least marginally competitive—though frankly without Evan's skills, it would have been dog meat. Gymnastics meets seldom attracted much of a crowd—people were more interested in the "big" sports: basketball, football, and baseball—but this afternoon the gym was packed. The bleachers had filled up early and latecomers were looking impatiently for seats. I guess people were morbidly curious to see if Evan would have the guts to show up. Or maybe they had turned out for the same reason that the Roman Coliseum had always been packed whenever the Christians were teamed up against the lions. Sitting and waiting, I was as jumpy as one of those Christians myself. Technically I wasn't disobeying my parents. I mean, it wasn't like I was hanging out with Evan; he was just one of the people who would be competing. But I guess I was afraid someone would see me and tell my parents I had been there. And they would wonder why. And then the old man would put two and two together and come up with an odd number: ohmygod, my son's a faggot. Why else would he be at a gym meet where a notorious homosexual was one of the competitors?

So you can imagine how really glad I was when the Petersons showed up. And, of course, sat down right in front of me.

Gee, thanks, I told God. Thanks a lot.

Considering what happened at church, it had never occurred to me *they* would show up, although they normally did attend all the high school sports events. For in addition to looking like a recruiting poster for the Marine Corps, the pastor was a jock like my father. Unlike my father, though, he dragged *his* son to all the games with him. Maybe he thought watching athletes in action would make Benjie a real boy. Or maybe—since he always dragged Mrs. P. along, too—he just thought that the family that spectated together stayed together.

He looked surprised to see me.

"Well, hello, Andy-boy," he boomed. "I didn't know you were a sports fan." He sounded like Perry Mason cross-examining a witness.

"Uh—I'm not," I said, sweating under my T-shirt. "I mean, Mr. Metz said all of us kids should come to support the team."

Mr. Metz was the high school principal and, of course, he hadn't said any such thing. But I thought it sounded plausible enough when I had rehearsed the lie earlier. Now I felt my face turn the color of a tomato and I imagined a big neon sign above my head that said "LIAR" flashing on and off. The pastor just grunted, though, and started explaining to Benjie what all of the equipment on the gym floor was for. Mrs. P. smiled at me and patted my knee, and I felt awful, as if my lie had been a personal betrayal of her.

Fortunately the P.A. system sputtered to life just then and an electronic voice welcomed the spectators and began introducing the members of the two competing teams—US and THEM.

As each athlete was introduced, he bounded out

onto the floor and was greeted with a spattering of applause—not a lot, since latecomers were still arriving and yelling at friends in the bleachers, while others were streaming in from the refreshment stand with their arms full of Cokes and popcorn; everybody else was busy talking and laughing and generally settling in. Even so, when Evan was introduced, there was a moment's dead silence while everybody turned and stared, the way people do at freaks in a carnival sideshow. Then some moron asshole hollered, "Oh, Honey!" and a lot of people laughed. Evan ignored it; the next person was introduced and shortly after that, the meet got underway.

Pastor Peterson had been right. I *wasn't* a big sports fan. The only reason I had come this afternoon was because I felt Evan needed at least one friend in the bleachers. But to my surprise, once the meet got underway even I had to admit that gymnastics was interesting and exciting to watch, to see the kinds of choreographed control people could exercise over their bodies. And when Evan performed, it wasn't only interesting and exciting, it was amazing. It looked like he was flying without wings. Watching the magic, Benjie bounced up and down in front of me like a jumping bean, laughing and applauding.

The only good thing about sitting behind Pastor Peterson was that I could hear him explain to Benjie what was happening. For example, he explained what the judges (three old guys sitting directly beneath us in the front row) were looking for when they scored the individual performances. And he explained that the participant's point total in each event would be added to a team total, the team with the highest number of points winning, of course. With this knowledge I was as puzzled as Benjie when Evan finished his first event—the parallel bars—and, after briefly deliberating, the judges announced a score of 7.5, considerably less than the perfect ten it had looked like to me. The score became even more puzzling when the next contestant performed the same routine with no more than clumsy competence and got a 9.

Altogether, each of the six team members performed six routines. And a pattern quickly emerged. No matter how brilliantly Evan performed, he got no better than a 7.5. And the other kids, performing far less skillfully than he, got higher marks—even the poor guy who fell flat on his butt dismounting from the high bar got an 8. I could see that Benjie was bewildered by it all. He kept asking his father about the scores and the pastor kept explaining that the judges were professionals and that they knew what they were doing. "Maybe Evan isn't as good a gymnast as he thinks he is, son," the pastor said. He sounded very happy. And I realized that I hated him.

The final indignity came at the end of the last event—the floor routine. Evan had resolutely refused to be shaken by the judges' unfair scoring of him and had been getting stronger and more impressive with each routine. Now he was brilliant, his body moving like a coiled spring across the mat, bounding and rebounding, springing to impossible heights. Even the openly hostile crowd applauded grudgingly. He nailed his final landing and stood with his arms flung up as if making an offering to God.

The judges' score was a 5. "Contestant faulted," the announcer reported, his voice booming like Gabriel's trumpet over the public-address system. "He stepped off the mat at dismount."

This was such a blatant lie, I was speechless. The pastor wasn't, though. "Good call," he shouted, slapping his big, meaty hands together as if the judges were Solomon reaching a particularly brilliant decision. As if, I suddenly realized, they had done exactly what he had hoped they would do when he had brought his son to the meet: They had cheated Evan and tried to humiliate him.

Evan didn't look humiliated, though, just baffled, but when the team totals were announced a minute later and our team lost by five points, he finally looked really angry. And he finally protested. I was only six rows above the floor and I could see him talking angrily to his coach, who just shrugged and walked away. Evan looked at his teammates, who were seated together on a bench in front of the first row of bleachers. If he expected their support, he didn't get it, either. They just scowled at him as if it was his fault they had lost. He tried to talk to the judges then, but they ignored him, too, closing up their rule books and folding their scoring sheets into neat little squares like napkins that they had used to mop up something messy. Finally Evan looked up at the crowd as if appealing to a higher court.

And the crowd started booing—not at the injustice of the judges, but at Evan. Evan stood his ground stubbornly while first jeers and catcalls rained down on him and then a crumpled Coke cup that someone threw at him. It missed but the next one didn't. It was followed by a shower of wrappers and popcorn kernels and then someone threw a half-empty can of soda. It hit Evan in the chest like a stone and he staggered back, more in stunned surprise than pain, though he winced and rubbed his chest where the can had struck him. Then someone threw another can and it glanced off his shoulder. The crowd had started to yell now. And I realized it wasn't a crowd anymore; it was a mob. People were actually cheering whenever some new projectile hit Evan, who stood there in front of them, looking up into the bleachers as if he couldn't believe what was happening. I saw Mrs. P. look anxiously at the pastor and heard her say, "Do something; they'll kill him."

Her husband just looked at her and shrugged.

I don't know what would have happened—maybe they would have killed him like Mrs. P said—if, at last, another can hadn't hit Evan in the head. This one knocked him down; the crowd caught its breath and that's when Benjie had an attack. It started with a strangled scream that people all over the gym could hear in the momentary silence. Heads turned away from Evan and toward us. Then Benjie started making horrible, choking gurgles deep, deep in his throat. He tried to stand up, one arm stretched up toward the roof as if all the air from his lungs had floated up there and he was trying to get it back. Evan was forgotten as people began standing up, craning their necks for a better look at this fresh horror.

"Get the car," Pastor Peterson snapped at Mrs. P., "and bring it around front. I'll bring Benjie."

Mrs. P. leaped up and ran down the aisle for the nearest exit while the pastor gathered up his son, whose face was contorted by his painful gasping for the breath he still couldn't reach. For just a second the man didn't look like the pastor anymore but like any father who is overcome by terror that his little boy is going to die. He got to his feet and started urgently down the aisle. And, for some reason, I followed him.

Evan had struggled to his feet and was standing at the foot of the aisle. His forehead was bleeding, but he ignored that and reached out his arms as if they were full of air he wanted to give to Benjie, to help him breathe. The pastor turned his body half away as if he were shielding the boy from a predator and hissed at Evan, "This is your fault."

Evan staggered back as if the pastor had hit him in the face. Then he turned and, at last, ran off the floor in the direction of the locker room. No one but me saw him go. Everybody else was watching the pastor wading through the crowd with the now unconscious Benjie in his arms.

• • •

Later, after everyone had left the gym, I headed for the locker room myself. I had seen everyone leave . . . everyone but Evan. I stood at the door to the room, almost afraid to go inside for fear I'd find him dead on the floor. Because it seemed now to be the kind of world where people could be killed just for being different and no one would care. In fact, the killers would probably get a 21-gun salute. Statues of them would be erected in public parks and parents would name their firstborn after them.

"Somebody stole my clothes while I was in the shower," Evan said dully. I found him sitting alive but naked on one of the wooden benches in the locker room.

"I was surprised to find my clothes gone when I came out of the shower," he said as if he were reasoning with himself, "because the other guys on the team won't come into the locker room at all now when I'm here."

He sighed.

"There may be some sweats in the storage room on the other side of the hall," he told me. "Would you check? I think I've had enough attention for one day without having to walk home naked."

I found a pair of sweats where he told me to look and we talked while Evan put them on.

"I guess none of this would have happened today if I'd dropped off the team," he said. "Coach wanted me to. I guess he saw this coming. But I haven't done anything wrong. Why should I be punished? I'm the same person I was a week ago, and this crowd would have been cheering for me then. Of course, that didn't stop my boss from firing me, did it? The Bird-of-Paradise has flown the coop, as far as Evan Adams is concerned.

"Let's see." He started counting on his fingers: "I've lost my job, my mother's about to have a nervous breakdown, my brother won't speak to me, a mob throws things at me. People cross the street to avoid me. God, it's like I'm a leper, not a homosexual."

"What will you do?" I asked finally, my voice sounding shaky. For a fleeting moment I wondered if there were such things as colonies for homosexuals and if Evan would be sent to one of them.

"I don't know, Andy," he answered wearily. "Try to tough it out until I graduate—it's only two more months. And then go away, I guess—to a big city where people may be more tolerant. Or at least where they don't know me."

Take me with you, I wanted to plead. But, of course, I didn't. I was afraid to say anything. And I hated myself for that. But he must have seen something in my eyes. Because he smiled at me.

"Thanks for standing by me," he said.

"You're my friend," I mumbled. I didn't know what else to say. Because I didn't know how to tell him what I knew now: that I loved him. With all my heart.

He glanced at the door. "You'd better leave," he told me, "before someone wanders in here and finds us together and decides that you, too, are"—he made his voice deep and gave a dramatic shudder—"*one of THEM.*

"God," he added, looking at my face. "Don't look so sad. At least things can't get any worse."

He was wrong, of course. As we would both learn soon enough, things can always get worse.

• • •

I didn't see much of Evan during the rest of the week. It was Holy Week and I was busy putting the final touches on the pageant. There was another rehearsal before the midweek service and it was a disaster.

"Oh, well," Mr. Shelton said, slapping me on the shoulder. "You know what they say: bad wehearsal, good performance."

I shrugged. It didn't make any difference. Parents loved it when the kids messed up, especially the little ones. Awww, the adults said, like they were looking at a basketful of puppies. Aren't they cute!

Well, there'd be *lots* of awws this year. But I just didn't care anymore.

The next day was Maundy Thursday and that meant another evening service, though only a handful of people ever came to this one. But Mother and I were there and Mrs. P. with Benjie, who was home from the hospital. The Sheltons were there and Eddie, too, sitting in the front pew with his unruly red hair slicked down and his face looking so fiercely scrubbed I was surprised there were any freckles left. I almost felt sorry for him. I guess his mother would see to it that he wouldn't be missing any church services ever again; after all, somebody in the family had to be held up as a shining example of American youth now that Evan had become a notorious outcast. I even saw Eddie deep in conversation with Pastor Peterson after church and wondered briefly if he was asking for advice about enlisting in the Marine Corps. . . .

The next day was Good Friday. I always thought that was such an odd name for the day when Jesus had been crucified. But for kids it *was* a good Friday because school let out at noon and spring vacation started the following Monday. Everybody was a little crazy with excitement or spring fever and most of the teachers just gave up trying to teach and showed movies instead. It was like this every year so why did it seem somehow . . . *different* this time? Underneath the high spirits there seemed to be something a little . . . ugly. A little . . . dangerous. Kids congregated in knots in the hallway and talked a little too loud and made gestures that were a little too big. They seemed like cattle you see in western movies when the first flash of lightning flickers across the night sky. They shifted nervously from foot to foot and tossed their heads and seemed to show too much white in their eyes. I kept being surprised by the sunshine I saw streaming in through windows because it felt like it was night at noon and about to storm.

"ANDY!" It was Patti-with-an-i. Rushing up to me in the hallway before last period. Panting from running.

"What!" I said, not caring that I sounded annoyed. I was nervous enough without any dramatics from her.

"It's Evan," she gasped.

"What about Evan?" I demanded, trying to sound casual now and failing. But Patti was too upset to notice.

"Some of the boys," Patti said. "I heard them.

They're going to do something to Evan after school."

"Oh, Jesus," I said. "What?"

"I couldn't tell exactly," Patti answered miserably. "But they were laughing. We've got to warn him."

But it was too late. The bell was already ringing and I didn't even know what class Evan was in that period, and besides Mr. Sum, our algebra teacher, was poking his head out of the classroom and saying, "C'mon, you two. Inside this instant or I'll mark you both absent."

What could we do? We went inside. And all through class I knew exactly how eternity must feel to lost souls in hell.

When the final bell rang, Patti and I were out of our seats before the sound had died away. But at that we were too late. We ran through the halls looking for Evan and hearing the teachers we brushed past yell at us to slow down. But we couldn't find him anywhere. And so finally we left the building and then we found him. It was easy. All we had to do was follow a gang of kids, all of whom seemed to know exactly where "it" was going to happen —whatever "it" was. I guess Patti and I were the only ones in the whole school who had been left in the dark.

We followed the others to a vacant lot near school where a crowd of guys had already gathered. Evan and Eddie stood in the center like two characters in a play everybody had come to watch. The curtain had already gone up by the time we arrived. Eddie, flushed and excited, was speaking his lines loudly. So he could be heard in the last row of the balcony, I guess.

"Yeah," he was saying to Evan—but playing to the crowd for encouragement—"Pastor Peterson told me what they do to fruits like you in the Marines."

Some of the guys in the front row grinned in anticipation. Evan looked pale but calm. And when he spoke, it was so quietly that even people who had the best seats in the house had to strain to hear.

"Why are you doing this?" he asked.

"Because you're a faggot, of course," Eddie answered. As if he were making some kind of brilliant point and that was that.

"I'm also your brother," Evan said.

"Not anymore," Eddie shouted. He wasn't even pretending to talk to Evan now; he was talking to all the other kids. "No faggot is going to be *my* brother," he boasted.

"Okay," Evan said wearily. "So I'm not your brother. So good-bye." And he started to turn away.

"Oh, no you don't, faggot," Eddie snarled. And as if it were a signal, the crowd closed more tightly around the two and Evan was confronted by a solid wall of boys' bodies in any direction he turned. I realized uncomfortably that Patti was the only girl there. I started to whisper to her to go home but Eddie's voice drowned me out.

"We can't let you go until we make sure everybody knows you're a faggot. We don't want you sneaking around pretending to be straight and maybe taking advantage of trusting little kids like Benjie Peterson." Eddie sounded now like he had forgotten his lines and was wildly ad-libbing. But everybody seemed to think it was funny. They all had these big, goofy grins on their faces as they surrounded Evan, and it was like some crazy dream because the smiles didn't make any more sense than the words Eddie was babbling. The teeth in the smiles seemed to be all canines—the ones we use to rip and tear at flesh.

"The marines know what to do," Eddie was shouting now. "And that's what we're gonna do to you."

And suddenly I realized why Pastor Peterson had been talking to Eddie the night before, and I started to feel sick to my stomach.

"Don't ya wanna know what we're gonna do to you?" Eddie demanded.

"What?" Evan asked. He sounded so sad—almost as if Eddie had died.

"We're gonna cut all your pretty faggot hair off," Eddie crowed triumphantly. And he pulled a pair of scissors out of his jacket pocket and held them up so the sun reflected off the blades.

"That's enough, Eddie," Evan said. "You're not going to do that."

"Oh, yes, I am," his brother grinned. And for the first time I realized that a fifteen-year-old Norman Rockwell kid could look evil. He nodded and two of the biggest guys in the front row, guys whom I recognized as having graduated the year before, grabbed Evan's arms. Eddie stepped forward and the scissors flashed just as Evan jerked his head back. The handful of hair that caught in the scissors was ripped out of his scalp and the bald patch that was left quickly filled up with blood. Then things started to really go crazy. Eddie lunged forward holding the scissors up just as Evan ripped one arm free and threw it up, trying to knock the scissors out of his brother's hand. Instead, his flying elbow caught Eddie in the nose and more blood began gushing. Eddie looked so surprised that it was almost comical and if somebody had laughed, maybe things would have turned out differently. But nobody did and Eddie went from looking surprised to looking oddly . . . *happy*. There's no other word to describe it.

"Now you're really gonna get it, faggot," he said, and hit Evan in the face with his fist. Evan staggered back and the two guys who had been holding his arms let him go just as Eddie hit him again.

"Well, c'mon, faggot," Eddie said, breathing hard, "are you afraid to hit back?" Evan just looked at him and his face was even sadder now.

"Hit me," Eddie screamed, and slugged his brother again.

"Maybe he'll hit me," one of the other guys said. And *he* hit Evan.

But Evan refused to hit back. He stood quietly with his hands at his sides. And another one of the guys hit him and then suddenly a shower of blows was raining on him and I had this crazy thought. The sound of the fists against his body sounded just like the noise my old man made when he pounded a cut of meat to tenderize it. He had a wooden mallet with a metal face that looked like the cleats on a football shoe. Each time he swung it against the meat, he grunted. Thud, thud, thud. Grunt, grunt, grunt. And I could hear guys grunt and then I'd hear a thud and then a grunt and then a thud. And Evan was bleeding. But so still. It was Patti who was doing the screaming.

"Stop them, Andy!" she screamed, "stop them! They're killing him." She was shaking my arm as if she would rip it out of its socket. But I didn't feel it. Didn't she understand, I thought? If I try to stop them, they'll know I'm a faggot, too, and then they'll kill me. Why couldn't she understand that? I thought. And the air was filled with more grunts that made it sound as if the crowd of boys had turned into a herd of animals busily killing an outsider with hooves and horns. And there were more industrious thuds and grunts and thuds and then Evan went down and feet replaced the fists and Patti screamed, "Get out of my way, coward," and shoved me aside and threw her body on top of Evan's.

"Get off him, you fat pig," Eddie screamed, "or you'll get it, too." But Patti didn't move; she just lay there, her body covering Evan's. Shielding it. And Eddie kicked her in the side. And she grunted, too, but she didn't move and she didn't cry.

"Shit, Eddie," Billy Curtis said. "She's a girl."

"I don't care," Eddie said hotly, and he started to aim another kick at her. But Billy pulled him away.

"You're a faggot, too," Eddie screamed at him.

And Billy pushed him away as if he smelled bad.

"God," he said, looking disgusted, "you're nuts. Well, fuck you." And he walked away.

Patti's action had interrupted the savage rhythm of the beating and now Billy's walking away stopped it dead. It was as if everybody but Eddie suddenly realized that this wasn't a play after all. It was real life. And it was a real kid they had been beating. A real kid who was lying unconscious on the ground, which was turning red around him with his blood. No one actually said anything. But no one needed to. Everybody understood the play was over and they all started to walk away. Nobody looked at anybody else. Finally it was just Eddie standing there, looking at his bloody hands. And then he looked down at his unconscious brother.

"It's your fault," he said. "It's all your fuckin' fault." And then he, too, staggered away. And only the memory of him was left like a bad dream when you first wake up.

"WakeupAndywakeupwakeup." Patti was screaming at me. And I thought, oh, it was just a bad dream and I opened my eyes and saw the blood.

"Get help," Patti screamed. "Get help. Can't you at least do that?"

Oh. Okay. I could do that.

I ran for it. I ran and ran. What a good boy I was.

The police car almost hit me when I ran into the street in front of it. And then the two policemen couldn't understand what I was trying to tell them until one of them slapped me across the face and words started to come out of my mouth instead of the noises I had been making. And then one of them pushed me into the police car and we drove, siren screaming or was that me, to the vacant lot.

We found Patti there. She was sitting on the ground now, cradling Evan's head in her lap.

"Jesus Christ," one of the policemen said, looking at Evan's bloody and battered body. "What happened here?"

The other one picked up Evan, who was still unconscious, and laid him gently on the back seat of the car. And then they drove away with the siren screaming.

And me?

Oh, I ran, of course. I ran away then. I ran and ran because I couldn't bear to look Patti in the face.

•   •   •

And so it turned out that Patti was the brave one. And I was the coward. Me. Andi-with-an-i.

Although he was in critical condition for a week, Evan had begun to rally, and they said he would recover.

No thanks to me.

We prayed for him in church. We prayed for Eddie, too. He tried to kill himself. But he failed. And they sent him away. To some home someplace.

They called it a home, anyway.

The rest of the kids got away with it. The police

and the school officials called it mass hysteria. And anyway, Evan wouldn't press charges.

Patti was the brave one. And I was the coward.

I was afraid to look her in the face.

And ten days later I was still afraid to go to the hospital.

"Andy. Andy."

I heard footsteps behind me. It was Patty. The day after she stopped Evan's beating, she changed the spelling of her name. Back to the original. Patty with a 'y'.

I looked down at the ground.

"I'm sorry I called you a coward," she said. "I was wrong. They would have tried to kill you, too."

"No," I said, looking at the ground. "You were right. I am a coward. I might have been able to stop it. But I was afraid."

"Don't blame yourself," Patty said. "Evan doesn't."

I looked up at her then. And saw that she had pretty eyes. Behind her glasses. I'd never realized that before.

"Why haven't you gone to the hospital to see him?" she asked.

"Afraid," I said.

"He's not mad at you," she said.

"That's not what I'm afraid of."

"What then?"

"I'm afraid people will find out I'm a homo sexual, too."

There. I said it.

"Oh," Patty said. Just like that. "Oh. Are you?"

"I guess," I said miserably.

She looked at me for a minute.

"Maybe you should talk to Evan about it."

Patty was smart. She was brave. And she was smart.

I went to the hospital. I stood in the doorway of Evan's room.

He was asleep.

My heart was pounding so hard in my chest I was afraid its sound would wake him up. But it didn't. So I went into the room and sat down in a chair by his bed and looked at him.

The hair was starting to grow back in the bald patch. His bruises were turning from purple to yellow-green. Most of his upper body was covered with bandages. I saw his chest rise and fall gently under them as he breathed. His eyes fluttered open.

"Hey," he said.

"Hey," I said.

We looked at each other.

"You've lost weight," he said.

"I haven't had much appetite."

"You can have my Jell-o when they bring lunch," he said. And he smiled at me.

That did it. I started to cry. Not little sniffles but great big, gasping sobs. I put my head down onto the bed and cried and cried.

"It's all right," he said gently. He put his hand on my head. "It's all right."

"No, it's not all right," I said when my voice came back. "I might have been able to stop them. But I was too afraid to even try."

"I was afraid, too," he said.

"But it was different with me," I said. And then I told him what I had been afraid of. What I was still afraid of.

"Poor Andy," he said softly. "It's not easy

growing up when you're different, is it?"

"No," I sniffed. And then I pleaded: "What am I going to do?"

"You're still so young," Evan said. "What are you? Fifteen? Give it a couple of years and see how you feel then."

"Take me with you," I said suddenly. "When you go. Take me with you."

He laughed and then winced and touched the bandages across his ribs. "It only hurts when I laugh," he said.

"I'm serious," I protested. "I love you."

The words that had been so hard to say wouldn't stop now: "I love you. I wanted so bad to tell you last Saturday when I came to your house. But I was afraid to."

"You shouldn't ever be afraid to tell someone you love them," he said gently, his hand stroking my hair.

"Then take me with you," I begged. "That's all I want. Just to be with you."

He took my hand. And I almost started to cry again.

"I can't, Andy," he said. "They'd say it was kidnapping."

"Not if I went of my own free will."

He put his hand under my chin and lifted my face up so I could see his smile. "I don't think your parents would feel that way," he said. "And besides, you *are* too young. Too young to know your heart. Yet. Maybe we should have this conversation again in three or four years."

"But you'll be gone," I protested.

"Maybe I'll come flying back," he said. He squeezed my hand and put it back down onto the bed.

And I realized that part of the conversation was over.

"Now tell me about the Easter pageant," he said, firmly changing the subject. "Did you get a standing ovation?"

And so we talked about stuff that didn't mean anything until it was time for me to go.

And when I came back for another visit three days later, determined to talk about important things again, he was gone. His bed was stripped and fresh linen lay folded at its foot.

"Oh, yes," the nurse at the station down the hall said, "he was released yesterday. Such a nice boy. Is he a friend of yours?"

I ran to the pay phone in the lobby. I dialed Evan's number and a recorded voice told me what I didn't want to hear.

I hung up and realized that your heart really does sink sometimes. I picked the phone up again and called Patty.

She sounded like she'd been crying. "They're gone," she said. "Pastor Peterson called Daddy last night to tell him and to ask Mother if she would play the organ for church until we can find a new organist."

"Where did they go?"

"I don't know," Patty said miserably. "Evan wouldn't tell me."

My confused silence asked the question before I could find the words.

"Yes," she said. "He stopped by the house yesterday afternoon. He claimed it was to say good-bye to me but I think it was really just to leave a package for you. I think I'm jealous," I heard her say as I dropped the receiver and ran for the hospital exit.

I ran all the way to Patty's house, where she was waiting for me at the front door. With a package in her hands. And an envelope. She handed them to me and she smiled.

"I'm dying to see what he gave you," she said, "but I expect you'll want to open these in private."

"Yes, thanks," I said, grateful for her understanding and surprised at how much she had grown up—in such a short period of time.

I started to walk away and then turned back. "Maybe," I said, "we could be—well—friends."

"Yes," she said. "I'd like that."

"I'll call you," I promised.

And then I couldn't wait any longer. I ran. But not far. The Sheltons lived only a couple of blocks from Evan's old house, which was dark and empty now, but I sat on the front porch anyway and ripped the paper off the package.

It was the angel wings. He had finished them for me. The feathers were white and pearl gray and they were very beautiful.

I ripped open the envelope. There was a note inside. This is what it said:

Dear Andy,

Maybe these will help you to fly.

I love you.

Evan

(aka GUARDIAN ANGEL MAN. Tah-dum!)

I put the note into my pocket and held the wings against my chest for a minute. Maybe so my heart could get to know them.

And then I started trudging down the long hill toward home. Gradually, perhaps unconsciously, I began to walk faster. And faster. And faster still. Until I was running full out. And then I slipped them on and spread my now wing-covered arms and the wind rushed under them and I leaped off the ground, and for a second I seemed to soar, to leave the earth behind me. To fly.

But then I fell. And pitched head over heels down the steep slope before landing on my stomach and sliding over the patchy grass and the dirt and the rocks to a final stop.

And then I simply lay there, facedown, the tattered ruins of the wings fluttering from my arms.

I got up finally, slowly and painfully. My right trouser knee was torn and I had grass stains all over the front of my shirt. I took the wrecked wings off and tucked them under my arm. I couldn't fly . . . yet.

But I could fix the wings. And I could run. And so I did.

With Evan's note in my pocket. And wings on my feet.

Andy in Love

Andy in Love

Professor Hawthorne can be a real bastard. Classes end Tuesday afternoon before Thanksgiving and the University shuts down from Wednesday through Sunday, but it's no secret that a lot of kids cut their Monday and Tuesday classes to extend the holiday.

So on Friday, Professor Hawthorne casually announces if anyone is contemplating a sabbatical next week, they should be forewarned that "the evil Mr. Stevenson" will be taking attendance and is prepared to do unspeakable things to anyone he finds absent. Everyone knows it's Professor H. who will be the doer of unspeakable deeds, not Mr. S., and so, though there's a lot of grumbling, no one dares cut. And then, to add insult to injury, Hawthorne gives us a pop quiz on Tuesday. It's only one b.s. question asking us to "discuss considerations of culpability in Hawthorne's *The Scarlet Letter*," something he's been lecturing about the whole week before, so it's no big deal but judging by the sighs and paper rattling going on around me, you'd think it was the end of the world.

Finally a girl sitting two rows in front of me timidly raises her hand and waves it at Stevenson, who is parading up and down the aisles to make sure the children don't cheat—so much for treating us like adults. He doesn't see her hand but the professor does.

"Yes," he says shortly, "what is it?"

The girl looks like her wildest nightmare has just come true.

"Oh," she stammers, "it's just—I mean, well, I just had a question for Mr. Stevenson."

The professor's face gets *that* look—the one a hungry predator gets when it spies prey that's trying to hide from its teeth and claws.

"That's all right," he says smoothly, "let *me* try to answer it."

And like prey that knows it's been discovered, the girl's nerve breaks and she stammers, "I—I don't—actually I don't know what this word 'culpability' means."

And the professor pounces. "You what?" he demands, making her repeat her confession.

I'd tell him not to play with his food but he's obviously enjoying himself too much to listen.

"God in heaven," he roars, "didn't you hear a word I said last week? All I talked about was culpability; if you didn't know what it meant, why didn't you look it up? Too busy shopping?"

"I'm sorry," the girl stammers, "it's just . . ." her voice trails off into lip-trembling nothingness.

The professor looks at her in disgust now. "Someone tell her what it means," he orders, and goes back to the book he has been reading.

And there is silence. Dead silence.

The man looks up, intrigued. There's more prey than he had thought. He doesn't quite lick his chops but he does raise one eyebrow.

"It means," Stevenson starts to say, but the professor stops him.

"Not you," he says. "Them."

And a lazy wave of his arm makes us all his prey now.

He leans casually against his lectern and surveys the silent room. "Am I to believe," he acidly inquires, "that there is no gallant able to define 'culpability' for milady? Could it be true, as I have heard it rumored, that all of your brains really *are* in your lances?"

There is some nervous laughter and the girl begins to cry quietly.

I can't stand it.

"It means blame," I mumble.

"What's that?" he demands, elaborately cupping his ear with one hand. "Did I just hear something?"

"It means blame," I repeat, louder this time.

His darting eyes find me and pin me, like a butterfly to a board.

He stares at me as he asks someone, "what's his name?" His eyes won't let me turn my head to see who he's asking but I know it's Stevenson even before I hear the T.A.'s voice reply, "His name is Logan."

"No, no, you must be mistaken," the professor says sardonically; "surely the name is 'Lochinvar.'"

"It says 'Logan' on the seating chart," Stevenson says dryly. Professor Hawthorne ignores him, continuing to stare at me.

"Well, Mr. Logan," he says; "if you really wish to impress the damsel, you'll tell her who this Lochinvar chap is, as well."

The girl has turned around in her seat and is staring at me sullenly, as if it's my fault this is happening.

"Lochinvar is the hero of a ballad by Sir Walter Scott," I tell her, only I'm looking at Professor Hawthorne. "He rescues his true love from the wedding hall before she is forced to marry another.

> *'So faithful in love, and so dauntless in war,*
> *There never was a knight like young Lochinvar.'*

I quote the last two lines of the ballad—the only ones I can remember, frankly, but I don't admit that.

"Great scott!" Professor Hawthorne exclaims, droll now. "Very impressive; I'm sure you've won the young lady's kerchief with your erudition."

The girl looks knives at me instead of scarves before she turns back to face the front of the hall.

"See me after class, Mr. Logan," the professor says airily and suddenly I'm the one who feels like prey flushed from its hiding place, my mind so busy with thoughts of escape I can't concentrate on the test and an easy question turns into the riddle of the goddam Sphinx. I finally give up trying to think and scribble down a bunch of stuff off the top of my head and finish just as the bell rings. The rest of the kids stampede to the front of the hall, toss their test papers at Stevenson, and gallop out the door into the liberating sunshine of vacation. Yippee!

I get up and walk slowly to the front of the now deserted room, a condemned man who hasn't even been given a hearty meal.

Professor Hawthorne is talking to Stevenson but breaks off at my approach.

"Ah, Mr."—there is the slightest pause and I think he's forgotten my name already but at the last second he recovers it—"Logan." And I'm suddenly oddly elated; hearing him say my name is like hearing a king conferring knighthood: Rise, Sir Logan.

"A very impressive performance," he says, looking at me closely. "What level are you?"

I'm not sure what he means but fortunately Stevenson answers for me: "He's a freshman."

"No!" the professor sounds incredulous now. "Where on earth did you get your secondary education?"

I name my hometown high school.

"Ah," he says, "I smell a small-town outsider who spent his lonely childhood in the company of books. Sound familiar, Mr. Stevenson?"

I glance at the T.A. "Yeah," he says tonelessly, "we're a dime a dozen, we outsiders."

"So, Mr. . . . Logan, hustling off for a good old-fashioned Thanksgiving in the bosom of your family?"

"No, sir," I answer.

"No?" he repeats, raising his eyebrows in an elaborate show of surprise. When you talk to him in person, I realize, his gestures are a little too large; it's like having a conversation with an actor who is playing to the last row of the balcony.

"Going home with a friend, then?"

I feel like the pop quiz has turned into an oral exam I'm going to flunk with my next answer, but I can't lie to God.

"No, sir."

"What's this?" he demands. "Alone on Thanksgiving?" He's looking at me now the way a biology student looks at the frog it's dissecting.

"Yes, sir," I say miserably.

"Well, Mr. Logan, we seem to be companions in solitude. I had expected to be out of town for the holiday but had to change my plans at the last minute. So you'll come to my house for Thanksgiving, and we'll provide each other company."

It sounds more like a summons than an invitation, I think—if I can think at all, I'm so stunned.

"Come by around one o'clock," he tells me. Then, glancing at his watch, says, "Speaking of the time, I must run. I'm having cocktails with the president."

And I wonder if he means the President of the University or of the United States. With him it could be either—or both.

"Mr. Stevenson, give the boy my address. Oh, and you'll have to call Fred and tell him he'll be fixing Thanksgiving dinner after all—for two. He'll have a fit over the short notice, but it can't be helped."

And without saying good-bye, he turns and walks briskly away.

I look after him, feeling like I've been hit in the head with a hammer. I guess that's how you feel when, without warning, a cherished fantasy turns into reality. Next he'll be asking me to call him "Christopher," I gloat, feeling as if I'm floating away on a soft, pink cloud.

"Lochinvar my ass," Stevenson snorts, shooting holes in my cloud. "Puh-leeze."

"What's wrong with you?" I ask, puzzled by his outburst.

He doesn't answer. Instead he starts stuffing test papers into his briefcase.

He acts like I no longer exist and so I start to turn away, saying awkwardly, "Well, have a nice Thanksgiving."

He stops me with a word: "Wait."

Still not looking at me, he mumbles, "Don't go to his place for Thanksgiving. Come home with me instead."

"What?" I sputter, wondering what the hell is going on with all these unexpected invitations. "I—I can't do that."

"Why not?" he demands, looking up at me sharply now.

"I hardly know you."

"And Hawthorne is your dear personal friend?"

"It's not the same thing," I protest, and, "anyway," I add, "I can't turn down *HIS* invitation."

"Then I'll turn it down for you," Stevenson says, sounding almost eager now. "I'll call him tonight and tell him you're not coming."

"But I *want* to go," I insist, wondering why he can't seem to understand that. I struggle to explain but all I can manage is a lame: "I mean, he's—he's *Christopher Hawthorne.*"

"And what does that make me, a piece of shit?" Stevenson demands, sounding furious suddenly.

I stare at him openmouthed.

"Oh, go to hell," he tells me, grabbing his briefcase and striding to the door. "Have dinner with your big hero. I don't care." He rips the door open, slamming it against the wall, and a thunder of sound rebounds from the back of the hall.

Stunned, I stand there in the sudden silence for a moment and then, "Gee, thanks," I tell the empty doorway. "You have a nice Thanksgiving, too."

• • •

The prospect of having dinner with my own personal god quickly turns from anticipation to agony. All I can think about is what might go wrong. I'll wear the wrong clothes; I'll use the wrong fork, I'll say the wrong things; I'll show up at the wrong time; or worse: I'll show up and find that Professor Hawthorne has forgotten he'd invited me. I get so nervous that on Thanksgiving morning itself I wake up at three and have to force myself to stay in bed until five when I finally get up and go for my run.

Of course, this means I'm back in the dorm, showered, shaved, and dressed, and ready to go by ten o'clock. By eleven I have to shower again and change clothes, since I've sweat through my first outfit. This time I put on a sweater to cover the perspiration half-moons that rise under my arms the second I put my shirt on.

I leave the dorm about noon and because Grandma Logan always taught me to take a present to a host or hostess, I stop at the campus florist and buy a bouquet of flowers I can't afford. I regret my choice of gift immediately, since it makes me look like I'm picking up a date for the junior prom instead of going to dinner at a famous professor's house.

I arrive fifteen minutes early and so I have to walk around the block about twelve times, sure that the rich neighbors will see me, decide I'm casing the area, and call the police. And then Stevenson can come and bail me out and have the pleasure of saying, I told you so. Shit!

At exactly one o'clock I ring the doorbell.

After what seems like an hour the door is opened by an elegant-looking man of about sixty. He's wearing a shirt and tie, a crisp white jacket, black slacks, and gleaming black shoes. He has very short gray hair and the palest blue eyes I've ever seen. He examines me with them and then sees the flowers I'm carrying.

"For me?" he says caustically. "But we've just met."

I can't tell if he's kidding or not—he looks like his idea of fun is doing horrible things to small animals—and so I start to explain, with sweaty seriousness, who they're for and who I am but he interrupts me.

"I *know* who they're for," he says. "And I know

who you are, too, Mr. Logan. Give me some credit. The professor is expecting you, of course."

He moves aside and I step into a house more beautiful than I could ever imagine.

"You may wait in the library," Gray-Hair says. "That's the first door on your left.

"Your left side is the one with the watch on it," he adds helpfully, as I start blindly in the wrong direction. I turn around and he stops me: "But do give me those poor flowers before you strangle the last bit of life out of them."

He pries them out of my hand.

"I'll put them in water," he tells me, and heads off toward the back of the house while I head obediently in the right direction this time, thinking I might as well faint and get it over with. I step into the room and discover I haven't fainted; instead I've died and gone to heaven.

I look at the bookcases and think immediately of Uncle Charles's room but this is twice as big and it's two stories high! In one corner there's a little circular staircase that rises to a balcony and a second level of built-in bookcases that fill three walls.

A massive wood desk and two leather chairs stand in front of the fourth wall, which is covered with framed photographs—of famous authors, I see, as I move closer to look at them and see they're all inscribed "to Christopher."

"You've discovered my rogue's gallery," a voice behind me says, and I whirl around to find that Professor Hawthorne has come quietly into the room. He's wearing an elegant blue blazer with a crest on the pocket, an impossibly-white shirt open at the throat, and gray flannel trousers. His loafers, which gleam like the desk next to me, have tassels.

"I'm sorry," I stammer, "I didn't mean to snoop."

"Don't apologize," he tells me; "all of *that* lot enjoy being looked at.

"But then so do I," he adds, giving me a dazzling smile.

My face does its tomato imitation and, "I love your television show," I gush. "I watch it every Sunday."

"A fan," he says, looking pleased. "I'm SO glad I invited you to dinner." His voice sounds now like the purring of a big cat.

"I—I brought you some flowers," I add, since I suspect Gray-Hair has thrown them away and I want the professor to know I'm a dutiful guest as well as a fan.

"Yes," he says, "Fred told me. That's very sweet. You obviously have beautiful manners."

And he gives me the same mocking half-bow he always gives Stevenson.

"But look at me," he says, "I'm forgetting mine altogether, keeping you standing here. Let's go into the sitting room, where we can be more comfortable."

He nods me through the door, putting one hand on my back to gently guide me down the hallway. I offer a silent prayer of thanksgiving that I'm wearing a sweater, since I can feel trickles of sweat making zig-zag patterns down my sides.

We enter a smaller room, comfortably furnished as promised, and with a cheerful fire blazing. We sit down together on a sofa as Gray-Hair enters the room carrying a tray with glasses and a silver ice bucket containing a bottle of wine.

"Ah, Fred," Professor Hawthorne says. "Impeccable timing, as always."

To me he says, "If you'll promise not to tell the

sheriff, I thought we might have some wine before dinner."

Gray-Hair puts the tray down on a table next to the professor and unsmilingly asks, "Should I bring a straw for the young man?"

"I think a glass will do very nicely, thank you," the professor replies, adding, as the man leaves the room, "dear old Fred. I inherited him from my parents and I'm afraid he gets a bit bored running this quiet house of mine—he's accustomed to managing embassies instead. My father was an ambassador, you know."

He hands me a glass of wine, asking, as he does, "Do you prefer to be called Andrew or Andy?"

I tell him "Andy."

"Very good," he says. "And I'm Christopher, in this house, of course.

"Happy Thanksgiving, Andy," he smiles then, as we clink wine glasses.

"Happy Thanksgiving . . . Christopher," I say, managing not to spill my wine as I leap through heaven's gate once more.

· · ·

Half an hour later we're on our second glass of wine and I'm feeling fine. I've just finished telling my close personal friend Christopher all about my close, personal . . . uncle—Charles.

"Ah," Christopher says. "Now I know where you get your love of books. Our Mr. Stevenson, who seems to know a *very* great deal about you for *some* reason, tells me you're a runner as well as a reader."

I nod into my wine.

"Though I might have guessed that, from your appearance," he continues. "I'd say you have a lean and hungry look but I'm afraid that if I did, you'd start quoting Shakespeare at me."

"Yond Cassius has a lean and hungry look," I dutifully recite. "He thinks too much; such men are dangerous."

Christopher laughs. "There, you see; what did I tell you? But no more thinking today. You're on holiday, Cassius. Time to relax and enjoy."

And he refills my wineglass just as dear old Fred appears in the doorway. I give him my biggest smile.

"Soup's on," he announces in a voice that makes me hope he hasn't fixed anything that curdles.

• • •

Christopher is relentlessly charming throughout dinner. He tells me a complicated story about German songs called lieder and a "dear friend" of his named Dietrich Fischer-something-or-other, who, he says, is the world's leading performer of the songs. And then he actually sings one that he calls his favorite!

He has a great singing voice and part of me knows he's showing it off for me, which makes me feel flattered and embarrassed at the same time.

"Look at you," he says, finishing the song; "you've hardly touched your food. No wonder you're so thin."

"I'm sorry," I apologize; "I guess I'm not very hungry."

"You're a very intriguing young man," the professor says. "I wonder just what it is that you *are* hungry for?"

I don't respond, although my famished heart knows the answer to his question, even if my mind doesn't. It's love I'm hungry for—*starving for*—and I think, now, that Christopher is, too. And so it is that when he comes around the table after dinner and stands close to me, I get up and gladly melt into his arms and turn my face up to be kissed. . . .

* * *

I wake up the next morning with the first hangover of my life. If this is the way the old man feels every day, I think with a groan, it's no wonder he acts like such a bastard. I roll over onto my stomach and put the pillow over my head to block out the light that is cascading noisily through the window.

I lie there, thinking about yesterday. . . .

Christopher's reaction when I put my arms around him was not exactly what I expected.

"WHAT THE HELL!" he thundered. I felt his body go rigid, as if it had just turned into a marble statue of itself.

"What the hell do you think you're doing?" he demanded.

"I, I, I"—I was sputtering like a boiling-over teapot. "I thought you were going to kiss me."

"I was just going to pour you some more wine, you idiot. Christ!" He sounded disgusted and pulled away from me so rapidly I lost my balance and fell against the table, knocking over a half-full glass of red wine; I watched the stain spread across the linen table-cloth like a birthmark, desperate to look at anything but his face.

"This is how you repay my hospitality?" he hissed, "making some cheap faggoty pass at me? What in hell could you have been thinking of?"

How could I ever tell him that I had been thinking that perhaps he might love me? I couldn't and so I said nothing, which seemed to make him even angrier.

"I want you to leave my house," he ordered shrilly. "Immediately. You're not welcome here any longer. Brazen little bastard."

There was no gentle hand on my back to guide me

now. Instead it was his words that, like sharp-toed shoes, seemed to kick me to the door and out of his house.

At the door itself, though, he stopped me with more words.

"For the record," he said, still furious but icy cold now, even though I could see his hands shaking, "I am NOT a homosexual. And if this has been some cheap, feeble attempt at blackmail or something equally despicable, understand that the university has ways of dealing with that. Do you understand?"

"Yes, sir," I managed to whisper.

"And for Christ's sake," he concluded roughly, "if the police should stop you on the way home, don't tell them where you've been. Drunken slut."

And he slammed the door behind me and turned off the porch light, leaving me standing there alone in the swiftly descending darkness.

♦   •   •

I spend the rest of the holiday somewhere in the no-man's-land between heartbreak and terror. My last chance for love is gone, my heart keeps blubbering; no one will ever love me now. And all the time my mind is shouting at my heart to shut up. Fuck love! my mind snarls. Think about what'll happen if you get expelled for making a pass at your professor. What then? Your life will be over.

I frantically try to remember exactly what Professor Hawthorne had said about the university's dealing with "that" but I can't; the fear has numbed my memory—the part that shame hasn't already eaten away, that is.

Somehow I survive the long weekend; classes resume and, superficially, everything seems the same as before. Except I now sit at the very back of the lecture hall when I go to Professor Hawthorne's class. I can't bear for him to look at me. Not that I have to worry because it's obvious he will look everywhere but the place *I* happen to be.

Stevenson, though, keeps shooting little question mark looks at me and each time I dodge them—and him, too, when he tries to talk to me after class. But I can't get away with that forever and he finally catches me, grabbing my arm as I try to sneak out of the room, surrounded by a bunch of other students.

"Hey," he says.

"Oh," I say, trying to sound casual. "Hi."

"So how was Thanksgiving with the great Hawthorne," he asks, "was it . . . divine?" He tries to make it sound caustic but for some reason it sounds anxious, instead.

"It was fine," I say, sounding as anxious as him because he's looking at me like I'm the scene of the crime and he's Sherlock Holmes.

"Uh, listen," I say before he can ask anything else, anything . . . *incriminating,* "I'm gonna be late for my next class. I'll talk to you later."

I pull my arm loose and before he can stop me, off I run, heading automatically not for another class but for the track, instead, where I run and run—to escape Stevenson's questions, yes, but also to try to outrun the memory of my awful Thanksgiving. But no matter how fast my legs move, it's always there, right at my heels—side by side with the equally painful memory of why it is I couldn't go home for the holiday. . . .

My Father's Scar, Part ii

My Father's Scar, Part ii

By the time I was a senior in high school, the old man was drinking too hard to keep a job. And so as his world hurried toward night, my mother had to go to work—as a checker in a supermarket. She hated it, and it showed in her face and the defeated way her shoulders drooped and the hump that started to form in the middle of her back. Always taller than the old man, she seemed shorter now. He had cut her down to size, at last. Most days when I got home from my run after school, she was still at work and the old man was already passed out and snoring—sometimes on his bed but usually on the couch in the living room. The TV would be blaring, tuned to the Westerns he liked to watch—the ones where the bad guys wear black hats and the good guys wear white hats, and the good guys always win. Maybe the old man needed to see somebody win, in a world filled with disappointment and defeat. I would stand in the twilight and watch him sleep, looking at his red face, his scar, and his mouth with its full lower lip and corners turned down in an angry-at-the-whole-world scowl. How rich in rage he was. My mother and I could not afford to be angry, though; we were too emotionally impoverished. And because we were poor in material ways, too, I did my best to help make ends meet. I started tutoring kids, referred to me by Mr. Elmore, the bow-tie-wearing high school counselor who knew I needed the money. He was a nice man but I didn't want his compassion. I had *earned* the right to teach other kids: I was a straight-A student, a brain, it was called back then in the sixties. And while I didn't expect the kids I tutored to be grateful for my help—they were paying me, after all—I did wonder why most of them seemed to resent me, as if I were a summer school teacher or somebody who had been put on earth just to spoil their fun. Their attitude put an even greater distance between me and them than the running did.

The only one who seemed to like me was a junior girl named Melissa, whom I tutored in English. She was over six feet tall and she carried her height like a curse. None of the boys would date her because she was taller than they were and none of the girls wanted anything to do with her, either, as if her unpopularity was a contagious disease. Sometimes, uninvited, she would sit at my table in the cafeteria, while the other kids avoided us both like the plague.

"You run a lot, don't you," she asked one day while idly moving the chili mac around on her plate with a fork.

"Yeah," I answered. "I guess."

"How much?"

I shrugged. It embarrassed me to talk about it. "Six to ten miles a day, maybe."

"That's why you're so thin," she said, giggling and sounding embarrassed herself. Her face was pointed down at the plate but her eyes were looking up through their lashes at me. "You remind me of the actor in that British movie, *The Loneliness of the Long Distance Runner*. I saw it on TV last weekend. What's his name— Tom something."

I wasn't paying much attention. Since I hadn't invited her to sit with me, I guess I felt I could be rude to her. Or maybe I was being rude to her because everybody else was. It was a trap you fell into, if you weren't careful. And in a way, she seemed to expect it. She didn't even react to it, just kept talking and looking at me, while I stopped listening and started looking idly around the cafeteria, not even paying attention to what I was seeing until I realized I was looking at Billy. Only he was no longer just Billy. He was now The Great Billy Curtis. The star quarterback. The hero of the football team. After his father died when we were fifteen, he and his mother moved away for three years but he was back now, a senior like me, and nobody's reflection; he shone now with his own spectacular light. He was sitting at a table on the other side of the cafeteria, surrounded by his groupies—lesser jocks and two or three of the prettiest girls in our class. He looked like a mountain peak surrounded by foothills.

And he was looking back at me. His eyes were like magnets holding my gaze to his. It was the first time I had looked directly at him since we were twelve years old.

"Tom Courtenay, that's his name," Melissa said. "You remind me of him, you're both so intense. Oh," she giggled, "I made you blush."

"Don't flatter yourself," I snarled, angered by the sudden confusion Billy's gaze caused. Getting up, I pushed my chair back so hard it fell over with a bang.

"Well, excuse me," Melissa pouted.

But I was already on my way out the door.

After that, whenever I saw Billy, it seemed our eyes would lock. We never spoke, though there seemed to be something long unacknowledged behind his eyes that needed to be said. Or maybe that was just my imagination because, frankly, I wasn't even sure he knew anymore who I was. As for me: Now that a bad memory was turning into a human being again, I discovered I was curious (maybe morbidly so) about the person Billy had become, so I started studying him the way I would a school subject. I worked from the outside in. For starters I was surprised to realize he wasn't that much taller than me—maybe half an inch—which would put him just over six feet. He seemed much larger partly because he outweighed me by about thirty pounds but more importantly because of his carriage. He wore T-shirts and Levi's mostly and when he walked, you could see the muscles move under his clothes—like the muscles under the velvet skin of a tiger. His short hair was tawny and there was something dangerous about him that enlarged his space. Maybe it was his screw-you arrogance. Or his anger. He had a terrible temper and people who followed sports said it was the only problem with his game, something which, unchecked, might keep him out of college football. Sometimes he would lose control on the field. The referee's whistles would blow, flags would fly like confetti in a parade, and a penalty would be called. And the newspaper accounts the next day would be full of scandalized stories about Bad News Billy, as the moron reporters loved calling him. Maybe Billy wasn't a mountain after all, I thought, but a volcano ready to erupt.

I was about to find out.

• • •

One day after school, I was leaving the building for my lonely run when the football coach, Mr. Lugg, stopped me. He was about as sensitive as his name or the tank he was built like, rolling relentlessly over any opposition. A former football player himself, he now had a whole team of little moons to reflect glory on him. No wonder he got paid more than the principal.

"Logan," he said, and I was surprised he knew my name, "Logan, the school needs you." It was the kind of rah-rah thing he said at pep rallies so I should have expected it but my reply was a stupefied "huh?" In my whole life no one had ever needed me before, and now a whole school did?!

"Elmore tells me you do tutoring," the coach continued.

"Yes sir," I said, regaining some composure and cynically wondering if he needed help balancing his checkbook.

"Well, we got a problem." Before I could even ask who "we" were, he went on: "You know who Billy Curtis is" (I nodded)—"well, Billy-boy is a genius at calling plays but off the field he's failing English and has a D– in trig. Get the picture?"

I got the picture. If the Einstein of the gridiron failed one class, he'd be suspended from the team for a whole grading period. If he failed two, he'd be off the team for the rest of the year and without Billy the team was nothing. Coach Lugg had a problem all right. But so did Billy. If he got kicked off the team, Bad News Billy would be yesterday's story, a former football player even before he got out of high school.

"Look, Mr. Lugg," I said, deciding I could afford to be sarcastic, "it's nice to know the school needs me but

I don't tutor kids because it's my patriotic duty. I get paid ten bucks an hour."

"Jesus, kid," Lugg said, "you're a real prince. Remind me to nominate you for the citizenship award."

When I just looked at him, the man said, "Okay. I'll tell you what. If you get Billy through those two classes, I'll pay you twenty an hour."

When he said "two," he jabbed me in the chest twice with a big forefinger as hard as a bullet. It hurt and I winced. The coach smiled at that.

The next day I had my first session with Billy Curtis.

* * *

We were to meet at four o'clock in the coach's office, a large room stinking of sweat and stale cigar smoke. No one was supposed to smoke on campus, but rules didn't apply to coaches. Or to Bad News Billy, either, I guess, because he was late. Or maybe he was just showing me who was boss. Anyway, he breezed in about four thirty.

"So it's really you, huh," he said, looking at me. "Old Andy Logan. Boy, you've really changed."

"*You* haven't," I answered.

"Huh," he grinned, "why mess with success?"

He was trying to be cool but underneath his cocky veneer he seemed nervous, and I wondered why.

I decided to try to find out. "If you're so perfect," I said, "how come you're failing two subjects?"

"One," he corrected.

"One is too many."

"School bores me."

"Look," I said, "I don't care if school bores you and I really couldn't care less what you do with your life, okay? That's your problem. But here's something to think about, big man: High school doesn't last forever. And I don't care how big a hero you are in school. When it's over, it's over. And if you doubt that, ask my old man—if you can wake him up. He's probably passed out."

I was really steamed. Arrogant jerk. I was right. He *hadn't* changed at all.

"Okay, okay," he protested. "Lighten up, man. I know what I gotta do."

"Then let's do it," I said tersely, and opened the trig textbook. And we did. But it wasn't easy. Billy wasn't stupid, I discovered, although he'd never be a brain surgeon, but he was impatient and easily bored. And there was a . . . tension between us that made it hard to concentrate. It was unspoken but palpable. I would be correcting a paper he had written, and I would glance up to find him looking at me, his eyes full of unasked questions. I would look away and pretend I hadn't noticed. But I had and when I was running, I found myself thinking a lot about Billy and wondering what might be going on in his head.

After about two weeks I found out.

It had been a rotten day. The old man had been fired from a nothing, part-time janitor's job for drinking at work—gee, what a surprise—and was taking it out on Mother and me. You'd think I'd have been used to it by now, but I wasn't. When the old man got mad, I turned into a frightened, clumsy, twelve-year-old fat kid all over again. I even knocked over a glass of milk at breakfast.

"Christ," the old man shouted, "you clumsy simp."

"I'm sorry," I mumbled, looking at my mother in a mute plea for support. She just looked away. And then got up to get a dishcloth to mop up the spilled milk.

"Don't do that, dimwit," the old man snarled. "Let him do it. It's his mess."

"Don't talk to her like that," I said, and he slapped me.

"Oh, Harold," my mother sighed. And I ran out of the house, my face burning where the old man had hit me. I ran away from my father. Away from my mother. Away, away. But I ran too long and was late for school. My eye turned black where the old man had hit me; I snarled at Melissa when she asked me about it and made her cry and that made me feel like crap. I was so upset I screwed up a big history test in the afternoon. And then it was time to tutor the great hope of the Western football world.

As usual, we met in a vacant athletic department office that had been reserved for our exclusive use, as if Billy were Royalty. His Highness breezed in ten minutes late, slamming the door behind him and tossing his books on the desk. When he got a look at me, though, he stopped dead.

"What?" I demanded defiantly.

"Wow. Where'd you get that black eye?"

"None of your business."

"Was it your old man? Does he still kick you around?"

I glared at him. "That's REALLY none of your business. Shut up about it, okay?"

I thought that might make him mad but he sounded hurt instead.

"I was just trying to be friendly," he said meekly.

"I don't need your friendship," I told him.

"Look," he said, urgently now, "I know you're still mad at me about that—fight thing when we were kids."

"Don't flatter yourself," I said. "And it wasn't a fight. It was a massacre."

He seemed flustered. "But I'm really sorry. I mean, I've thought about it a lot. Things were lousy at home then and I guess I needed somebody, well, to take it out on and you" . . . his voice trailed off.

"And I was there to take it out on? A sissy fat boy who wouldn't fight back? How convenient."

I made it sound really sarcastic.

He hung his head. "I'm sorry."

"Oh, yeah?" All of a sudden I was shouting. "Well, maybe you should have been sorry six years ago. It's too fucking easy for you to just *say* you're sorry now."

I stood up. I was furious but confused, too. I wasn't accustomed to people offering me friendship, especially people who had made my life hell—even if it was half a dozen years ago when I was just a little kid. And I was confused, too, because this tentative, meek Billy wasn't the arrogant stud hero I thought he was. This Billy was more, well, interesting. And I was feeling something stir inside of me, maybe a . . . fondness for him I didn't want to examine.

"Where are you going?" he asked anxiously, standing up, too.

"Out of here," I raged. "You're too fucking stupid for me to help, anyway."

My body tensed to run but he looked so wounded I hesitated for a second, just long enough for three things to happen: I thought, Oh, Jesus, I sound just like my old man. I started to cry. And Billy lunged at me.

I cringed away, thinking he was going to hit me and I'd have two black eyes full of tears.

But he didn't hit me.

He kissed me.

Have you ever been surprised by a kiss? Really surprised? It's like being tackled so hard it knocks all the wind out of you. It leaves you gasping. His lips hit mine so hard, it was like he was punching me with his mouth. I recoiled so hard, in turn, that I lost my balance and fell down, like a fumbled football. He stood anxiously over me. "Oh, Jesus, are you okay? Did I hurt you?"

"No warning," I mumbled, rubbing my mouth with the back of my hand. Not trying to rub the kiss away— I couldn't even remember what it had tasted like. It had just been two hard lines with two rows of teeth behind them, hitting my mouth.

"I'm sorry," he said, frantically. "I don't know what happened. I just had to do it, y'know?"

"It's okay," I mumbled. But it wasn't okay. It was crazy. Not what he had done but what it had done to me. I was dazed. And dizzy. And the stirring of the moment before was turning into an earthquake that threatened to turn my life upside down. I hadn't felt like this since Evan left town three years before.

"Hey," he said, sounding worried, "are you sure you're okay?" He held out his hand. "Here, let me help you up." I took his strong football player's hand and he lifted me up as if I weighed no more than an empty uniform. I stumbled a little when I found my feet and he put an arm around me to steady me. We stood very close together. So close I could feel his breath on my face. And suddenly I was afraid to breathe. Was this the kind of tension *he's* felt in the closing seconds of a game, when he's called the last play, the play that will win or lose the game for the home team, team, team. And the whole stadium is suddenly hushed. Shhhh. Everyone is leaning forward in their seats in the stands—leaning closer and closer but so silent, afraid to breathe, afraid to damage the moment. And I was leaning in closer, too, afraid that I would mess up the play. I didn't fall this time, though. His body stopped my forward motion. "Oh," he sighed, as our bodies touched and the tension snapped, and his arms went up to catch—not the snapped football—but me. And this time there was no surprise. No fumble. Just wonderful, liberating release. It was a touchdown, and the home team won.

• • •

We found an abandoned house about halfway between our two neighborhoods and met there after school, spending long afternoons of sweet urgency, lingering each time until the last twilit moment when we absolutely had to go home or run the risk of arousing suspicion. We worried about that, of course, and were agonizingly careful never to go to the house together. Billy figured out half a dozen different routes and we alternated them, never approaching the house the same way on two consecutive days. Billy was good at figuring out that kind of stuff. It was the quarterback in him. Calling the plays. And that's why he said it first, I guess. He was calling the play: "I love you," he said.

Wow. Just like that.

"I love you," he repeated, and I knew he wanted to hear the same words from me in return. When I was silent, he looked at me with anxious eyes, and I saw his vulnerability again, the same vulnerability I had seen in the coach's office. And I felt so strong; it was the kind of rush I experienced when I got my runner's second wind. I felt invincible and I wanted to protect Billy from his secret vulnerability, from the world and the future and the past, and I wished there were dragons so I could protect him from them, too. And I rushed to reassure his anxious eyes.

"Me, too," I whispered, and was almost embarrassed at the relief I saw flooding into his face. Did I
deserve this? To hear the words, I love you. Words that
astonished my heart even though I didn't understand
what they meant. Didn't understand what love was. I
only knew it was that stirring feeling I had had for Evan,
a feeling that was wonderful and terrible at the same
time but incomprehensible—like angels, maybe. And
maybe that strange stirring was an angel opening his
wings inside of me. At night when I lay alone at home
in bed, I thought about this new feeling. Of wonder and
delight. And strength. Was love supposed to make you
feel stronger than another person? Was that why the
old man loved my mother—if he did? Because she
made him feel strong? If that was what love meant, I
didn't want any part of it. Don't need me, I wanted to
say to Billy, just to make me strong. But I couldn't.
Because I did need him to need me. I needed the luxury
of his love. . . .

●　●　●

In an odd sort of way I felt closest to Billy in the
guarded distance of school when I would pass him in a
hallway, surrounded by other kids, all of them rushing
to class, brushing shoulders, absently engaging in little
acts of physical contact that meant nothing to them but
everything to me when Billy would make a move and
engineer a little intimacy of our own and no one would
know except us. "Excuse me," he'd grunt impersonally,
squeezing past me in the crowded hallway and rubbing
his shoulder against mine. "No problem," I'd coolly
reply, and our eyes would lock for less than a second,
and tell each other, No one knows but us. This is our
secret. Our secret, special life. The second would pass,
Billy would swagger off, and I would risk a glance after

him, enjoying the looks of adoration the other kids lav-
ished on him. And I wanted to laugh because I was the
only one who really knew him.

To anyone watching, our lives would have
appeared unchanged. I still ran. Billy still played football. I continued to tutor him and we made some
progress. He actually started passing tests. Coach Lugg
slapped me on the back. "You're okay, kid," he said,
chewing on his cigar as if it were bubble gum. "Keep up
the good work. Here's a little incentive." And he slipped
me a twenty.

But something was different.

"Hey," Billy said one afternoon. "Are you happy?"

That was it. I was happy. "Yeah," I said, wonderingly, "I am."

"Me, too," Billy said simply, satisfied to leave it at
that.

But I couldn't, because I wasn't blessed with his
simplicity. For me it was something I had to think
about. And wonder at. And try to understand. I, Andy
Logan, former fat kid and object of scorn, was actually
happy. Had I ever been happy before? Maybe at
Christmas when I was a really little kid. Or when I had
spent those afternoons reading with Uncle Charles or
those mornings running with Evan. Maybe then but
never since. It made me almost uneasy to feel happy.
Why? Because being unhappy had seemed so normal
that it was almost comfortable? Because what made me
happy was being loved by another boy? I frowned at
that thought, because it was the first time I'd had it and
I didn't like it.

"You don't look it," Billy said.

"What?"

"Happy."

"Sorry," I said, "I was just thinking."

"You think too much," Billy said sternly. "You'll hurt yourself." He grabbed me and pulled me close. "Lighten up," he said in my ear. I relaxed against him. Such intimacy was never casual, it was too important for that, but it was becoming easier because each time it seemed more natural. More . . . inevitable. When I was with him in our abandoned house, I felt complete. Fulfilled. I felt that together we were a family. We were a world. *There* was a reason to be happy. So why did we have to keep such happiness a secret? Why should we be afraid to tell anyone or everyone? Because people thought it was wrong for two boys to be in love with each other? Or because one person, the old man, would think it was wrong? Queer. That was a shit reason.

I must have been frowning again because Billy had pulled away and was looking at me with a concerned frown of his own.

What the hell, I thought, let it go for now. Maybe the only answers were in feeling, not thinking. I smiled at him reassuringly and put my arms around him. He sighed in relief.

"That's better," he said, and smiled back at me, sweetly.

● ● ●

But, of course, I couldn't let it go for long. I'd spent too many years substituting thought for feeling to just stop thinking about us all at once. It was just too important. I thought and thought about it while I ran. But my thoughts never took me as far as my feet. And inevitably, I guess, it started to affect our relationship, this endless wondering about these new feelings, about this new me.

"Hello," Billy would call, waving his hands in front

of my face. "Earth to Andy. Come in. Where are you?"

"I'm sorry," I'd say, "I was just thinking."

"Look," he'd say, "if you want to be alone, all you have to do is tell me. I can go."

"No," I'd say, "don't go."

Then a few minutes later, when my mind had started to wander again, "Fuck!" he'd shout, "I'm outta here." And he'd storm off. And then he'd storm back and grab me and our bodies would take over and supply their own urgent answers. Then later we'd quarrel about other things, even though they weren't the real problem. I would nag him about studying and he would rebel. "You've gotta study," I'd lecture. "I don't gotta study," he'd sullenly reply. "But you'll flunk." "Who cares?" "I care: What'll happen when I go off to college and you haven't even graduated high school?" "I'll graduate." "But you can't afford to go to college unless you get a scholarship." "I'll get a football scholarship." "Not if you flunk out of high school." "Why don't you just give me one of your scholarships, then? You've got—what, four of them?" "Don't be stupid, I can't do that." "But I AM stupid, Andy; I'm just a dumb jock. I'm not smart like you, okay? You don't need to keep reminding me of it." And his temper would explode and he'd throw a schoolbook across the room.

Well. It was true he wasn't as smart as I was. At first that hadn't made any difference. If he hadn't needed help with his classes, we never would have gotten together, as I reminded him more than once. But it was a difference between us. I thought too much and he thought too little. And I wondered what he found in me to love. And another little distance entered our relationship.

And so I ran and I ran. If only, I thought, we could tell the whole world about us. If only. Somehow, in some obscure way, it seemed to me that would validate our relationship. It would validate me. It would give me an identity as a complete person, not some weirdo freak. And everything would be okay. Or would it?

Meanwhile, life went on. I now had scholarship offers from five different universities, including the one that, wonder of wonders, miracle of miracles, finally offered Billy a football scholarship. The day he got the news, we recklessly cut our afternoon classes and went to our house, to our home, and for that one afternoon everything was as deliriously wonderful and sweet as it had been at first. But wonderful is a word that describes moments, not lives. The school year was ending. And I found myself wondering what else might be ending.

• • •

Commencement. Billy called it "Andy's big evening." "An' here he is, ladies an' gennelmen," he would say in a really awful Ed Sullivan imitation, "the star of our reely big shew, Andy Logan." He was talking about the fact that I was valedictorian, and had to deliver the commencement address, which I did, feeling uneasy at being the center of so much attention, afraid the spotlight would reveal too much, and feeling awkward when the superintendent of schools solemnly shook my hand and presented me with a pin I knew I'd put into the back of a dresser drawer and forget. I collected my scholarships and got some tepid applause. But the biggest ovation of the evening came when Billy's scholarship was announced and he jumped and feigned elaborate surprise. His mouth dropped open. His hands flew to his face. Who me? Like a ham actor winning an Oscar. The audience loved it, laughing and cheering. Billy was the real star, but Coach Lugg gave me a clenched fist salute and a big wink (and a check after the ceremony. "Y'did it kid. You should be a teacher.") I applauded politely like a kid who hardly knew Billy but was tolerant of his shenanigans because he was a hero—I was getting good at that kind of sham.

Then it was over. Some of the teachers and a few kids shook my hand and congratulated me (Billy was not one of them, of course), and Mother and the old man were suddenly there. Mother kissed me on the cheek and, without crying too much, told me how proud she was of me. The tears ran down deep grooves on each side of her mouth, and I felt guilty because I'd never noticed them before. The old man shook my hand; he'd had a few, but he wasn't staggering or anything. "We're proud of you, son." The way he said it made it sound as if he hated me, but I guess that's not fair because I don't know what he was thinking. And I never will. He was scowling but maybe that was just because he was trying to see one of me instead of two. And then all of a sudden, Melissa ran up to us. Breathlessly, "Oh, Andy, I'm so proud of you." And kissed me. It wasn't a very good kiss because she was throwing her arms around my neck while I was still turning my head to see who it was and so her kiss caught only half my mouth and the bottom of my nose. She blushed bright red and said, "Well, my folks are waiting for me, bye." And she was gone. My parents were as surprised as I was. "Who was that?" Mother asked. "Just a girl," I said. "Melissa." "I don't think you've ever mentioned her, have you?" "She's one of the kids I tutor," I said. "Well," the old man said, "it looks like you've been teaching her something, all right." And he winked at my mother. This time I knew what he was thinking, and I started to say, "no, she's not a girlfriend or anything," but I stopped myself. I stopped myself because both my parents looked so—I don't know, pleased or relieved or something. And then I thought, how would they look if that had been Billy who'd just rushed up and kissed me. And I knew then I had to tell them. I had to tell them. And I almost did. I swear I almost did. But they left too soon. They went home.

"Don't stay out too late," my mother said (I had told them some kids were getting together). "Ah, let him alone," my father said. And suddenly, for the first time in my life, I saw myself as my parents must have seen me—this weird intense skinny lonely smart kid who had no friends, who didn't do any of the things normal kids did—only ran and read, ran and read, ran and read. Maybe I scared them, the way things we don't understand scare us when we're kids; the way my feelings for Billy scared me. After all, my parents didn't know me. They didn't know anything about me. But how could they? I didn't know me, either.

I was trying to explain this to Billy later that night, trying to make some sense of it, when he put his hand over my mouth.

"Please," he said, "please just let it alone for tonight, okay? This is our special night, okay? We just graduated high school. *I* just graduated high school. With a scholarship. You want to know who you are? You're the kid who made that happen. Can't we just celebrate that?" He'd brought a bottle of champagne. He popped the cork and filled two plastic glasses. "*This* is important, okay? To us." We clinked glasses and drank.

· · ·

"Oh, shit." It was my voice. Even before I opened my eyes I knew what had happened. "What?" Billy's sleepy voice asked. "Oh, shit," I said again. "It's morning. We've been here all night." I looked at my watch. "It's eight o'clock." In a panic now. "What'll my parents think?" "Screw 'em if they can't take a joke," Billy said thickly and stretched lazily. "It's not funny," I said urgently. "I gotta go. I'll talk to you later." And I ran out the door.

Eight o'clock. Maybe they're not up yet. It's Saturday morning, after all. Sometimes when he'd been drinking, the old man slept until noon. And my mother didn't have to work today. Maybe they're still in bed. Maybe. Maybe. Maybe.

But, of course, they weren't. They were in the kitchen. Sitting at the table, a cheerful patch of sun on the red-and-white-checkered tablecloth. The room was warm and smelled like coffee. A real all-American room. But my mother's face was pinched with anxiety. "Oh, Andy," she said. "Where have you been, we've been so worried." "So," the old man said, "did she give you your graduation present?"

The look he gave me was almost one of complicity.

"*Was* it that girl?" my mother asked. "Is that where you've been?" The sunlight was on her face, too, and it was cruel, like a spotlight revealing all her wrinkles and fret lines and gray hair.

"*Was* it that girl," she repeated, anxiously now.

So there it was: my out. My easy out. Just a little betrayal of Billy. And myself. And what we were together. Yeah, sure, wink, wink, nudge, nudge, she gave me my present all right—all night long. The gift that keeps on giving. Haha. My mother would be upset, of course, but the old man had taught me what she thought or felt didn't matter. And I could be a hero to him. My son is normal. He spent the night with a girl.

Yippee. Get along little dogies. Sorry, Daddy, I thought, and realized I hadn't called him that since I was twelve. I didn't call him anything anymore—not daddy, not father, not dad, not pop. In my mind he was the old man and that was all. Sorry, Daddy, your white hats aren't going to win this time.

I took a deep breath. "It wasn't a girl," I said. And the whole world seemed to hold its breath. "It was a boy. I spent the night with a boy. I'm gay."

And then time became discontinuous. It stopped flowing; it became a series of frozen, individual images I could examine at my leisure, like pictures at an exhibition. Oh, there's an interesting one, I might say, pointing at the image of my mother, looking at me with a puzzled little smile, struggling to understand what I meant and trying with her little smile to reassure not me but herself that it was all right. Everything was all right. Oh, that one's powerful, I might say, pointing at another: the old man looking stunned, like a bull that's been hit between the eyes with a hammer. Oh, and that one's me. I've just said, I'm gay. I wish I could say I looked proud or defiant or bold in the picture. I should, shouldn't I? I've just spoken the truth. I've put the truth into simple words of one syllable. I'm. Gay. I shall say the truth and the truth shall make me free. Or something like that. But I only look afraid. No, apprehensive. That's how I look. Wondering what the truth will really make me.

How could I have wondered? Life is so predictable in our little house with its all-American kitchen, so drearily inevitable. Time resumed its forward motion and began flowing, no, *cascading* to make up for lost momentum. My mother's hand flew to her mouth. "Oh, Andy, you don't know what you're saying. You don't understand what that means." My father started to get up and then fell back into his chair. His face was dead white except for the scar on his cheek. That was bright red. His features contorted and, for a moment, I thought he might explode. But the only things to explode were the words that erupted from his mouth. "Jesus Christ, a faggot, my son's a fuckin' faggot, oh, Jesus, get out, get out of my house an' never come back, never." The room was full of the sound of his words so loud I could no longer hear what my mother was saying, but I could see her lips move and I could read the words, "he doesn't know, he doesn't understand;" it looked like she was praying. I could hear the old man, though; he was sputtering now, speaking in words, not sentences—"Jesus, faggot, out." And I smiled a little smile because it sounded like he was performing an exorcism and I turned and I walked slowly out of my father's house, and I didn't look back. I didn't look back. Not once . . .

• • •

Billy was still in our abandoned house when I got there. "That was quick," he said, surprised, and then, getting a better look at me, said, "what's wrong." I smiled my little smile at him. "I told them," I said. "I told them I was gay." "What, what did they say?" he asked tentatively, as if maybe he didn't want to know. I remembered the words and spoke them: "Jesus, faggot, out." I grinned and wondered if my face was going out of control. "Huh?" he said. "He kicked me out," I said, "he kicked me out, out, out," and then my face did go out of control and the rest of me, too, and I started to laugh, a high, keening laugh but it wasn't laughs coming out of my mouth; it was screams coming out of me like hiccups and I couldn't stop them and I looked sadly at Billy and wished I could say I was sorry for scaring him but I couldn't stop the screaming long enough to say so but he was brave and strong and agile for me and he leaped up and grabbed me as if he thought parts of me might start flying off and he pulled me down to the floor with him and held me and made soothing noises at me and put a hand at the back of my head and pushed it into his chest and I could feel his heart beating there and maybe it was the rhythm of his heartbeat that soothed the screams and turned them into sobs and then he rocked me, back and forth as if I were a baby and said "it's okay, it's okay" over and over as if that would make it so and once I think he said "Jesus, what's he done to you" but I didn't have to answer because he wasn't talking to me and after a long time, exhausted, I fell asleep.

• • •

A door slams and I wake up. Billy comes into the room. A great rush of energy comes into the room before he does, though. And I think, Billy will never need drugs to get high. I mean, when he gets pumped with adrenaline, it can be scary—like during a football game—like now. He's so excited, so proud of himself he almost shines. He grins at me through his split lip. He tries to wink at me with his right eye, but it's starting to swell shut, and he winces and grins again. We look at each other. I know what he's done, and he knows that I know. "He fights pretty good, your old man," he says. "I think he likes to fight. But I don't think he liked it when I kicked his butt." He laughs and winces again. He touches the injured eye. There's a cut on the cheek beneath the eye. He'll have a scar there, I think.

Sometimes I wish I was an old man—not somebody's old man, just an old man, and that my life was nearly over so I could look back and be wise about things that had happened to me. But I'm not. I'm still a kid and I have to try to figure out what things mean and what is right. I hope I'm doing the right thing now. I get up slowly. I look at Billy and I'm sorry that this is the way I'll have to remember him, because I love him so much, and I'm proud of those feelings. But I ask too much of him, expect too much of him. We're too different, he and I. He can only be true to himself, after all, and I guess I've known that all along. Maybe, in an odd sort of way, I used that knowledge to set him up, to use him. I don't want to think about that right now because that would make me think too much about myself. I turn away and I walk out of the room. "Hey," Billy's voice follows me, "hey, Andy, where y'going?" I walk on. "Andy. Come back, Andy." But I can't and when I get outside, I start to run. And I don't look back.

Andy in Love

Andy in Love

After I've been running about half an hour I hear someone overtaking me and automatically move over so whoever it is can pass me on the inside. The other runner doesn't pass me, though; he just draws abreast and runs next to me. I glance over and almost break stride when I see it's Stevenson steaming along beside me.

He sees my surprise and protests, "Hey, it's a public track; it's not your private preserve."

I look away. Why can't he just leave me alone, I think desperately, and pick up my pace. Gamely he increases his, too. But before we've run two more laps, he's in trouble. I can hear his gasps for breath and I figure in another minute he'll drop out but instead he reaches over, grabs the back of my sweatshirt, and puts on the brakes.

"Hey!" I yell. "Lemme go."

He's bent double now, gasping for breath but holding on to my shirt as if it's glued to his hand.

"God," he wheezes, "and this is supposed to be good for you?"

A couple of other runners zip past us. "Gangway," one of them hollers over his shoulder.

"C'mon," Stevenson pants, "let's get out of here before somebody runs over us."

And he pulls me off the track.

"You're stretching my shirt," I whine. "Why can't you just leave me alone?"

"Because," he answers, still gasping for breath and looking at me like I'm his favorite charity, "I'm concerned about you. Look at you, you've lost about a hundred pounds and those circles under your eyes make you look like a raccoon with cancer. A raccoon with cancer *and* a stretched-out shirt," he grins sheepishly and lets go of the material.

"I haven't been sleeping very well," I mumble, tucking the shirttail back into my sweats.

"Are you sick?" he persists.

I shake my head and look away, out over the deserted football field, and I try not to think what a fool I am. It's been raining—a cold rain because it's early winter now. All the leaves that had been so beautiful have turned a dull brown and the rain has knocked them off the trees and stuck them together in moist clumps that look slick and shiny as if giant snails have been crawling over them.

I can feel Stevenson's searching look and I know he's getting set to ask me the big question. And, sure enough, he does:

"Something happened on Thanksgiving, didn't it?"

"No!" The word comes out too loud and, Stupid! I think to myself, why don't you just holler "Bingo!" and give him a prize.

"That's what I thought," he says, sounding as satisfied as if I had. "So what happened?"

I panic.

"It's none of your business," I blurt, and then try to go on the offensive: "Besides, what do you care? The last time we talked, you told me to go to hell."

I had meant to say more, but I stopped suddenly because, hearing my words, I realize that that's exactly where I have been. In hell. And I understand, more powerfully than I ever have before, that hell is being totally alone, completely solitary, a place I have been for so many years of my life that I can't stand it anymore I.

Just. Can't. Stand. It. So I take a deep breath and share with him what happened. I open the door to my confidence and let him in. And I guess maybe in some other dark corner of my mind I hope it'll make him feel all sorry for me and that he'll tell Professor Hawthorne how much I'm suffering and the professor will take pity on me, too, and not have me expelled or cast into the outer darkness or whatever dire thing he's planning for me.

So what does my hero, my confidant, Mr. Stevenson do? He laughs! He laughs so hard he has to bend over and hold his knees.

"Well, thanks a whole hell of a lot," I huff. "Here I'm dying and you laugh like a madman."

"Oh, honey," Stevenson howls, "I'm sorry. I know it's not funny to you but I'm trying to imagine what Hawthorne's face looked like when you puckered up."

He wipes the corners of his eyes with one hand and grabs my arm with the other, as tight as if his tears of laughter were going to sweep him out to sea if he doesn't hold on.

"I'll try to remember how funny this is when Hawthorne has me expelled," I say stiffly.

"What?" Stevenson demands, grinning wolfishly. "Hawthorne? Expel you? And run the risk of having someone hang a big 'S' for 'Scandal' around his neck? He'd sooner die. Expelling you is the last thing he'd do. In fact, I guarantee you, you'll get an $A+$ in the class, just to make sure you go quietly.

"Trust me," he adds, patting my arm reassuringly as I continue to look dubious.

For about a second I feel better but then I remember how infatuated I have been with Professor Hawthorne and how painful and humiliating his rejection has been. And I try, brokenly, to explain it to Stevenson:

"I thought—I mean, I really thought he might be in love with me. I needed that . . . so much."

"I'm sorry," Stevenson replies, more seriously now. "But, boy, did you get the wrong number. I'm afraid the only guy HE'LL ever be in love with is the one he admires in the mirror about a thousand times a day."

"But why did he invite me to dinner?" I demand. "And why did he come on to me the way he did?"

"Because he's a monster," Stevenson says simply. "His ego is like a baby bird. It has to get fed about ten times its weight every day to survive. It flirts shamelessly to get adulation like yours. But, see, it doesn't have to be *yours,* specifically. It could be another boy's. Or a girl's. Sex has nothing to do with it. It's just nonspecific, undemanding worship that it needs. YOUR big mistake was expecting something from him in return. Give something back? That's the idea that stampeded him. It must have been like telling a baby it has to replenish the mother's milk it's been sucking up. Unheard of! As long as he gets what *he* wants, he doesn't care how much other people might be depleted or even hurt."

"I'm such a moron," I say bitterly. It seems so obvious when he explains it that I feel cheap now and used—like a Kleenex that someone has blown his nose in and thrown away.

"No you're not," Stevenson says gently. "I wouldn't like you so much if you were a moron."

I look at him blankly.

"You just don't get it, do you?" he asks. "Why do you think I got so mad when you were all starry-eyed and swooning over having dinner with the great Hawthorne?"

When I shrug, he says, "Because I was jealous, dummy! I couldn't stand it that you had this big crush on him, when he doesn't even care that you're alive, and all the time, I'M the one who's in love with you!"

"What?" I manage to gasp before my dumbfounded jaw drops to the ground.

He leans forward to speak directly into my ear: "I'm in love with you," he repeats, slowly and deliberately. "I have been ever since I saw you smile in class that day."

And then, leaning back and seeing my face, he cracks, "Geez, I guess you missed that, huh? Better let me help you pick that jaw up off the ground before somebody comes along and steps on it."

He bends over and pantomimes picking something up.

I barely hear him. A huge confusion of feelings is suddenly stampeding through me like a herd of buffalo and I look at him wonderingly, as if it's the first time I've ever seen him—and maybe it is because then I'm remembering the Sunday school lessons Mrs. P used to teach about all those people in the Bible—the ones whose eyes are covered with scales that suddenly fall away so they can see that the stranger they have been walking with is actually Jesus or an Angel of the Lord or something like that. And I remember Pastor Peterson raving about homosexuals waking up and finding themselves in hell and I begin to think I've woken up to find myself in heaven. And it isn't my eyes the scales have fallen away from, it's my heart, and suddenly I can see ITS reasons at last, and I realize that what has been disguised as anger or hatred is actually love. Love. I can't believe it.

Stevenson is looking at me now like he can read me thoughts.

"Hello, love," he says, smiling softly at me.

"Hi," I answer awkwardly as he reaches out and pulls me gently toward him. I don't resist; I just lean against his body, which is still a stranger to me but familiar, too, like an old friend you've learned something new about. I rest my head on his shoulder and find it's a perfect fit.

And there we stand for all the world to see, halfway between the track and the football field, and I don't care because it feels so right to be where his arms are.

And then I have a thought: "You know what?" I tell him. "Here I am in your arms and I don't even know what your first name is."

"Oh," he says. "That!" He sounds reluctant as he says, "Okay, I'll tell you but you've got to promise not to laugh."

"It's not 'Mister,' is it?" I ask, grinning against his shoulder.

"No, stupid," he says affectionately. "It's . . . 'Sascha.' My crazy mother named me that. She's Russian and she thinks she's the Queen of the Gypsies. Hey!" he slaps my shoulder. "I told you not to laugh."

"I'm sorry," I say, "I'm not laughing about your name. I love it. I'm laughing because I think I just got a sign."

And I send a silent "thank-you" to Evan, wherever he is. And I hope wherever that might be that he's as happy as I am right now.

Sascha holds me gently in his arms and I realize something else: that it's not me who's Lochinvar, after all; it's him. He's the one who's galloped to the rescue and it's the circle of his arms that is to be *my* castle, keep, and sanctuary, as warm and approving and welcoming as ever Uncle Charles's rooms were. I see it so clearly now. I sigh in contentment and marvel at how all those years of running in circles have somehow, miraculously, brought me to the right place at last.

"Welcome home," Sascha whispers, and we smile . . . together.